FIVE HOLIDAY TALES

DARA GIRARD

CONTENTS

"Something New," Copyright © 2013 Sade Odubiyi; "A Cup of Cheer," Copyright © 2012 Sade Odubiyi; "New Year's Surprise," Copyright © 2012 Sade Odubiyi; "A Mother's Day Wish," Copyright © 2012 Sade Odubiyi; "A Fortunate Mistake," Copyright © 2013 Sade Odubiyi;

FIVE HOLIDAY TALES

Copyright © 2013 by Sade Odubiyi

ISBN: 978-1949764659

All rights reserved. The reproduction, transmission or utilization of this work in whole or in part in any form by any electronic, mechanical or other means, now known or hereafter invented, including xerography, photocopying and recording, or in any information storage or retrieval system, is forbidden without written permission.

Printed in the United States of America

Cover photo © lightsource/depositphotos

Cover and Layout Copyright © 2022 ILORI Press Books, LLC

This is a work of fiction. Names, characters, places and incidents are either the product of the author's imagination or are used fictitiously, and any resemblance to actual persons, living or dead is entirely coincidental.

ILORI PRESS BOOKS, LLC

P.O. Box 10332

Silver Spring, MD 20914

www.iloripressbooks.com

ALSO BY DARA GIRARD

Collections

Domestic Disturbance (written as Dara Benton)

The Lady Next Door and Other Stories

Holiday Hearts

School Days: Five Story Collection

Lost and Found

5 Holiday Tales

10 Holiday Stories

Henson Series

Table for Two

Gaining Interest

Careless Rapture

Dangerous Curves

Familiar Stranger

Clifton Sisters

The Sapphire Pendant

The Amber Stone

The Emerald Ring

Novels

Honest Betrayal

INTRODUCTION

I love the holidays. Not just the ones in the fall like Thanksgiving and Christmas, but the ones in the spring and summer as well. So instead of just gathering Christmas stories for this collection, I decided to mix it up a bit with a Mother's Day tale, a New Year's Eve tale and a story about Thanksgiving.

This collection starts with "Something New" a Thanksgiving story about a woman who has to decide what the season means to her.

In "A Cup of Cheer" a shop owner finds holiday romance with the curmudgeon next door.

In "New Year's Surprise" a woman attends a party and learns to trust her heart again.

"A Mother's Day Wish" is a spring tale about a teenager who has to fight his family's bad reputation to get the chance he deserves.

And finally "A Fortunate Mistake" is a magical Christmas story about a woman who learns that the past has a lot to teach her about the future.

I hope you'll enjoy reading these holiday tales as much as I did writing them.

Dara Girard
December 2013

SOMETHING NEW

All Lewa Olunlade wanted for Thanksgiving was a turkey and her sister's husband. At thirty-four she dreaded going home for the traditional family gathering where people would laud her sister's excellent 'catch' and bemoan Lewa's single state. She could already imagine what "the Aunts" would say. Although not related by blood, Lewa called them her Aunts out of respect and cultural norm which acknowledged both their ages and that they were close family friends.

"You must stop being so picky," Aunty Elizabeth would say.

"I had two children by your age," Aunty Femi would add with a note of pride.

"The further you're past thirty, your chances of a good husband dwindle to nearly nothing."

"Unless you want a divorced man."

"And he'll probably have children."

"And who wants to raise someone else's children?" Aunty Elizabeth would say with a ring of superiority and distaste, having made herself an expert on men, marriage and childrearing. Although she'd twice had her face rearranged by her husband's fists, no one ever spoke about it because at least she was married and had two wonderful children. At sixty, she'd left her husband in Nigeria, who was now using his fists to beat his mistress and his four children by her, and she was finally free to use the power of being a married woman without having to deal with all the realities.

Aunty Femi had three children who basically tried to ignore her existence so she spent every holiday with the Olunlade family instead. None of her children felt it necessary to include her in their holiday gatherings since she was on the southern East Coast and they had all decided to settle in the northern region. They sent her money to assuage their guilt for their shoddy treatment of her and occasionally an email or a brief phone call, but little else. Lewa could guess that her children were likely embarrassed by their mother's loud coarse ways-- her English was poor and her table manners worse. However, Lewa knew Aunty Femi had a good heart and could understand her parents' affection for her. Aunty Femi's marriage had been fine, she'd been a widow for ten years, but Lewa gave up trying to decipher what 'fine' meant although she had on a number of occasions asked Aunty Femi if she'd been happy. Aunty Femi would only reply that she'd been married and leave it at that.

Lewa understood the underlining truth behind every word and glance of the Aunts and her mother: It was better to have a husband--no matter how wretched-- than no husband at all. It was a woman's fate. And she was arrogant and naive to expect any better.

"Caring for another man's children isn't so bad, if the woman isn't around," Aunty Femi would say to continue the conversation. She liked to talk and the topic of marriage and children made her feel smart.

"But then again, a woman isn't meant to be alone, so a divorced man is better than no man," Aunty Elizabeth would add and the Aunts would nod and continue to talk about her as if she wasn't there, because in a way she wasn't. A single woman in her family amounted to only half a woman. Not even a woman, half a person. Lewa could only hope that soon the talk would shift back to her sister, who'd been married three years but still hadn't had a child.

It had surprised everyone that by the end of the first year of marriage she hadn't introduced a new family member, preferably a boy, of course, but a girl would suit as well. After the first childless year, Lewa's sister, Arielle, had just laughed at the teasing, but Lewa could see the strain in her sister's eyes and plastered grin with each passing year.

Maybe this year she'd announce the news her family expected to hear. Lewa could imagine her sister and her husband, Stillman, making good parents. Stillman hit the marriage tri-fecta--family from the upper echelon of Nigerian society, Oxford educated with another degree from Yale and a respectable career as a biomedical scientist. He was solid, respectful and smart. A son-in-law any family would be proud of with skin the color of roasted chestnuts, and a smile as bright as Broadway lights. He was very charming and, on more than one occasion, Lewa wished he was hers. As a beverage scientist, she had a career she was proud of and a number of friends, but Stillman was one of the few individuals she felt easy with. But Lewa knew that her sister's marriage was solid and kept her fantasies to herself and briefly wished she didn't have to see the happily married pair this year. Besides, she didn't want another year of jollof rice, curried trout, plantain moi moi and pepper soup. She wanted a turkey like millions of other US families--even vegetarians celebrated with tofu that at least tasted like turkey.

Two weeks before Thanksgiving, Lewa listened with awe as her friend, Valerie, a fresh faced blonde from Wisconsin, described her upcoming feast while they sat in the cafeteria of their office building.

"Mashed potatoes, turkey, and cranberry sauce."

"What's the cranberry sauce for?" Lewa asked.

"It goes with the turkey."

Lewa didn't understand but nodded anyway. "Okay go on."

"Just the usual," Valerie shrugged, not understanding her friend's interest. "Cornbread, stuffing, ham, green beans."

Lewa sat back in her seat and sighed. "That sounds heavenly. I wish I could just be a fly on the wall."

"Would you like to come over?"

She sat up with interest. "Really?"

"Sure, we'll have plenty of food and I know my family won't mind."

"Perhaps you should ask your husband first."

Valerie laughed. "As long as he gets food, he doesn't care who shows up. I'm hosting his parents and trust me we'll have leftover for days." She grinned warming to the idea. "Yes, you should come. It will be fun."

Lewa sat back her hope slowly dwindling. "I'll think about it."

But she didn't have to think about it. Lewa knew she would have to ask her mother and she already had a good idea of how she would respond.

'No." Mrs. Olunlade said as she checked over the shopping list for the upcoming feast. They sat in the kitchen while their housegirl, Biti, carefully cleaned the special holiday dishes. Her mother was a small woman with delicate features that belied the mind of a sharp woman who had a successful nursing career and been married thirty-six years to a man who treated her well.

"But Mom. I've been invited."

Mrs. Olunlade did not look up from her list. She scribbled a note down. "And you can go another time. Thanksgiving is for family."

"But--"

She lifted her gaze and pointed her pen at Lewa. "And this time your grandmother will be able to join us. Would you want her to come all the way from Nigeria and not see you here?"

"She could see me on another day."

"She will see you on Thanksgiving." Mrs. Olunlade

returned to her list, making it clear the discussion was finished.

Lewa sighed exasperated. Her mother could be as unmovable as a stone castle. "Then can we do something different this year?"

Mrs. Olunlade looked at her daughter suspicious. "Different?"

"Yes."

"Such as what?"

Lewa took a deep breath, then said in a rush. "Can we have a turkey?"

"For what?"

"To eat." Lewa tapped the table hoping to make her mother understand. "Mom, that's what people usually eat during Thanksgiving. A big delicious turkey. You've been here long enough to know that."

"But we always have curried trout and I thought you liked my seasonings."

"I do."

"And Aunty Elizabeth makes jollof rice."

"Yes."

"And Aunty Femi makes moi moi--"

"Mom, I know." Lewa sat forward and clasped her hands together, trying to show a piousness she didn't feel. "It's just that...just this once I'd like to have something different."

Mrs. Olunlade frowned. "I don't know how to cook a turkey."

"We could follow a recipe," Lewa said with a note of hope.

Mrs. Olunlade set her pen down and folded her

arms. "Why are you worrying about food when you don't even have a husband to show your grandmother when she comes?"

Lewa fell back like a lead balloon. "You're changing the subject."

Mrs. Olunlade lifted her daughter's chin, her gaze softening. "You're so pretty and bright. What am I supposed to tell her?"

"You don't have to tell her anything."

"Mrs. Adeniyi has a son."

"No."

"You can't leave everything up to fate. The problem with you is that you haven't made it a priority and before you know it, it will be too late."

"I'm only thirty--"

Mrs. Olunlade quickly covered her daughter's mouth as if she'd said something foul. "Quiet. You don't look it and there's no reason to keep saying it. Do you think being over thirty and unmarried is a virtue?"

Lewa removed her mother's hand and kissed the back of her palm. "I'm sorry. I'll be more careful next time. Now, what about a turkey?"

Mrs. Olunlade's mouth quirked up in a quick grin, sensing her daughter's strategy to appease her. "I'll think it over. Go ask your father and see what he says."

"Dad, can we have a turkey for Thanksgiving this year?" She'd found him in the family room watching a NOVA special. She sat in the chair opposite him.

Mr. Olunlade was a large man with a soft spoken voice and his voice was even softer now. "What did your mother say?" he said with a note of caution.

"She told me to ask you."

He nodded then said, "How's work?"

"It's fine, now about the turkey--"

"Are you seeing anyone?"

Lewa blinked looking bored. "Dad."

"Does that mean no?"

Lewa shook her head. "No, I'm not seeing anyone, but I--"

"Why not? Why haven't you found someone to settle down with yet? You're a pretty woman and--" He pointed at her. "You must be doing something to scare them off. Do you tell them how much you make?"

Lewa affectionately squeezed her father's knee. "Dad, stop changing the subject. Can we have a turkey or not?"

He rubbed his chin, hesitant. "What did your mother say again?"

Lewa sighed, praying for patience. "She wanted to know your opinion."

A slow grin spread on his face. "That's rare. That means she's not sure. I say no. Let's stick with tradition."

"But that's my point. Jollof rice, moi moi and curried trout isn't traditional for Thanksgiving. Other people at least have a turkey."

"I don't care." He held up his hand like a feudal king making a decree. "It's the tradition for this house and it means a lot to our family. Do you know why we have jollof rice with curried trout?"

"No."

"Because trout was the first expensive meal I could afford. When I first came to this country I worked in a gas station. I hadn't met your mother yet and I stayed with Big Mummy's family. Finally I was able to get a promotion and the first thing I did was go to the local international store and purchase trout. So every Thanksgiving I buy that to remind me of how thankful I am."

"WHAT DID YOUR FATHER SAY?" Mrs. Olunlade said catching Lewa trying to sneak out of the house without saying goodbye.

"He told me a story about why we have jollof rice and trout."

"So his answer is no turkey?"

"Yes, he wants to keep our tradition."

Her mother beamed. "Good, but I've decided you're right. We should add something extra and I spoke to Femi and she's going to cook something you'll love."

"Really?" Lewa said clasping her hands together.

"Yes, she'll make samosas."

Lewa's hands fell to her sides. "But Mom that's Indian."

"Yes, exactly," her mother said pleased with her cleverness. "Didn't the English eat with the Indians?"

Lewa stood for a moment wondering if she should laugh or cry. "Yes...no...not East Indians. They ate with American Indians. Native Americans."

But her mother had stopped listening. She adjusted the collar of Lewa's coat. "She's excited because she knows it's one of your favorites. See, I do listen and can be flexible."

Lewa sighed. "Thanks Mom."

Mrs. Olunlade called the housegirl, Biti, and handed her the list. "I want only the best."

She bowed appropriately submissive. "Yes, ma'am." Although only nineteen, she looked ten years older and had stooped shoulders.

Lewa kissed her mother on the cheek then left.

Once she and Biti were both outside, Lewa gently slapped the younger woman in the back. "How many times do I have to tell you to stand up straight?"

"Sorry Aunty." She rubbed her hands together, and wrapped her scarf tighter. "I still have to get used to the cold."

Lewa glanced up at the red and yellow leaves clinging to the trees, feeling the crisp November air against her skin. "You weren't cold in the house, so stop lying."

"Sorry Aunty."

"Always stand tall." Lewa walked to her car.

"Aunty?"

She turned. "Yes?"

"Why do you want a turkey?" Biti asked making a face. "Isn't that just bland English food?"

Lewa laughed at the girl's expression, knowing she wouldn't understand. "Goodbye, Biti," she said then jumped in her car.

"Just forget about the damn turkey and eat what you're given," Lewa's friend Hannah Lee said as she, Lewa and Valerie changed in the gym locker after swimming. She'd known Hannah since they met at the university and could always depend on her for straight talk. "The holidays aren't meant to be enjoyed. If you're having fun, you're not doing it right. It's about family, fights and feasting. You just grin and bear it."

"I don't mind spending time with my family, and I don't mind them bothering me about a husband," Lewa said. "I've gotten used to it."

"You're braver than I am," Hannah said. "If I hadn't met my boyfriend in time I would have made him up."

"Yes, being single on the holidays is the worse," Valerie said.

Lewa rolled her eyes. "Thanks for your support."

"No, I don't mean you. I mean in general. It makes you an easy target."

"I can take being a target, if I could just get something different to eat. Is having a turkey so wrong?"

"It's not what they're used to," Hannah said. "We don't have mashed potatoes we have sticky rice."

Lewa rested her chin in her hand. "At least you have a turkey."

So it was clear. Thanksgiving meant many different things to different people. To Hannah it was sticky rice and family fights. To Valerie, a warm family gathering and traditional American food. To her father, jollof rice and trout reminded him of all he was grateful for. Thanksgiving was a symbolic day of family and blessings. Her parents had no connection to the story of turkey and mashed potatoes, and maybe she was grasping at a story that wasn't hers either. She needed her own special dish.

A week before Thanksgiving she bought a turkey.

"So what are you going to do with it?" her younger sister Arielle asked while the two woman stared at the frozen bird on Lewa's kitchen counter. "It's huge."

"I know." Lewa poked it. "And I'm not sure what I'm going to do yet."

"Why do you want a turkey so bad anyway? You can have turkey any other day."

"It's not the same."

"And why are you making it so complicated? If you wanted turkey why not just buy a cooked one?"

"Because I want to do it myself."

"You could get burned."

Lewa looked at her sister curious. "How could I get burned?"

"It happens every year. People get burned trying to cook their turkeys."

"That's only if they're deep frying them," Lewa said playfully hitting her. "Stop being so negative. If you don't want to help, why did you come over?"

"I'm curious."

Lewa lifted the turkey and put it back in the freezer. "I'm curious about something too." She closed the freezer door and looked at her sister. "Are you ever going to tell Mom and Dad about the miscarriage?"

Arielle sat down at the kitchen table and tugged on one of her braids with nervous fingers. "Why would I?"

"Then they won't bother you about starting a family." Lewa sat in front of her. "I know it must get on your nerves."

"I don't want them to blame me," she said in a choked voice.

"Why would they blame you?" Lewa said surprised by her sister's worry. "At least they'll know you're trying and they may be more sensitive."

"The Aunts won't be."

Lewa sighed recognizing the truth of her sister's words. The Aunts would be harder to convince. "You will have your own family soon."

"Aunty Elizabeth will blame me for not eating the right foods, Mom will say it's because I'm too old and should have started sooner." Tears filled her eyes.

Lewa covered her sister's hand. "But we know that none of that is true," she said in a soft voice. "You haven't done anything wrong. And you and Stillman will be fine."

Arielle brushed away her tears and lowered her eyes. "It's caused a strain between us."

"Of course," Lewa said giving her sister's hand a reassuring squeeze. "It's a stressful time for many couples."

"No, I mean...he's not handling it well. He's getting pressure from his family too and I'm afraid he'll start blaming me as well."

Lewa stiffened and sat back. "He's supposed to be your support not your judge. Do you want me to talk to him?"

Arielle lifted her gaze, suddenly wary. "What would you say?"

"Treat my little sister right or I'll punch you in the face."

Arielle smiled then laughed. "You're so silly."

Lewa returned her smile glad she could lighten the mood. "You're good together. You're a great couple. I don't want this to pull you apart."

"You can't stop it, if it does."

"It won't. "

"But what if I can never carry a baby? Sheba is already on her third," she said referring to a cousin of theirs.

Lewa brushed the idea aside with a quick flick of her wrist. "It's too soon to think like that."

Arielle shook her head. "No, it's not. I asked him and he said that if I couldn't have a child then we wouldn't have a marriage."

"He didn't mean that."

"He did."

"What about adoption or surrogacy?"

"He doesn't want to adopt and we can't afford surrogacy. Unless..."

"Unless what?"

"We could find someone to help us," she said looking at her sister with a hopeful expression.

Lewa shook her head, resisting the urge to jump up and run out of the room. "No way. Don't look at me. I'm not ready for that."

"This may be your only chance," Arielle said

suddenly eager. "You're older than me and we both know your prospects are slim."

"Thank you Mom," Lewa said in a sour tone.

"I just want you to consider it. If you could do this we'd both appreciate it."

LEWA LET her sister's words hang in her mind. Having a baby was something Arielle really wanted and if it could help her marriage it would be worth it, right? But then part of Lewa was angry that her sister had to find another alternative. Couldn't Stillman be more patient? Couldn't they come up with something together? Would he really leave Arielle if she couldn't bare his children? Would a child really change all that? Did he love her sister or was she just an appendage to him? A status symbol?

Lewa had to find out for herself so she met her brother-in-law at his office and treated him to lunch.

Once they'd placed their orders she said, "Do you love my sister?"

Stillman looked at her surprised and baffled. "You know I do."

"Then why are you threatening to leave her?"

He paused then said, "I didn't say that."

"Then what did you say? I know about the problem between you two."

He glanced around as if afraid someone might over-hear them. "Do we have to discuss this here?"

"No, we can go to your place and I can talk to you

with Arielle there. Or I can wait until Thanksgiving and let the whole family give their opinions."

Stillman held up his hands in surrender. "All I said was that having my own children means a lot to me." He let his hands fall. "It's something I've always wanted and it's expected."

"Dreams can change."

"Not this one. Being a father to my own flesh and blood is what I want."

"She really wants to have children with you. But can you love her enough if she can't?"

"We are thinking about surrogacy."

"Yes, she told me. And that hasn't answered my question."

"I don't mind doing that," he said expertly avoiding a question he didn't want to answer. "If she can't do it herself." His gaze trailed the length of Lewa.

Lewa took a sip of her drink. "Take the thought out of your mind and bury it."

He shrugged. "It's been done before and it would really help us a lot."

"I'm older than her."

"But you're better built to carry children," he said making a curving motion with his hands.

Lewa held up her hand and pointed at him, unable to stop a smile. "Watch it."

He grinned. "It's a compliment. If I hadn't met your sister first, maybe--"

Lewa laughed. "I used to think that too, but now I know it wouldn't have worked."

He frowned. "What do you mean?"

She shook her head, knowing she wouldn't be able to explain it to him. She was only starting to understand it herself. "I'll see what I can do."

"Arielle told me you bought a turkey for Thanksgiving."

"I'm not sure what I'll do with it yet."

"You'll come up with something." He winked. "You always do."

THAT EVENING, Lewa sat in her kitchen and pondered her conversations with Stillman and Arielle. And as she thought, she discovered a truth about herself too. That she didn't really want her sister's husband, just the status he brought her. She didn't want to get married--at least not yet. She was enjoying her life and truly never thought about being a wife and mother the way other women did. Her former desire for a husband had been a way for her to fit in. A way to stop being so different. It was the same with the turkey. She wanted their home to have the same sights and smells as other homes, but for what purpose? Was it wrong to be different?

Lewa loved Stillman. He was a wonderful, generous man, but she now realized he was more traditional than she'd thought--than she'd allowed herself to see. His values matched her sister's perfectly. Despite their easy conversation and ambitions, he would be a terrible match for her. She could only hope that the right man was out there. If not...her family would continue to feel sorry for her. She'd be a failure, a half person, but she didn't mind anymore because she had a private joy no one could take from her. A joy of being authentically herself. She didn't want her sister's private fears that she wasn't a complete woman if she couldn't bear children or Stillman's fears of how he'd be perceived. Even if they did have a child, Lewa knew it wouldn't be enough. They'd be expected to have at least two. To live others expectations could be exhausting and Lewa was ready to remove herself from that race.

Lewa called her sister. "Try for another year. If you're still having trouble, I'll pay for a surrogate."

"Thank you," Arielle said with tears in her voice.

"Just be prepared for the Aunts this year."

"I am. What are you going to do about the turkey? I think you should donate it."

"I could, but I'm not going to. We're having turkey this year one way or another. I'll see you Thursday." Lewa hung up then opened her freezer and stared at her frozen turkey with renewed determination. Authenticity, that would be her contribution to this year's holiday dinner.

LEWA WENT ONLINE and looked at different recipes and spent many hours looking at cooking clips. But she still didn't find anything that would suit her family. She decided to go to the store and stood in the baking section staring at the deep fryers, beakers and thermometers. She knew cooking was a science, but she felt like a novice in the lab of a genius. Even if she got the turkey right she didn't know anything about stuffing or glazing. She wanted to create something her family would eat, something familiar yet a little different. Unfortunately, she didn't know what.

"Can I help you?" a sales associate said. He looked like a college student and had shaggy red hair he kept having to push back from his eyes.

"No, I'm just looking."

"Okay," he said then started to turn.

"Wait," Lewa said before he left. "What do you do for Thanksgiving?"

He shrugged. "Watch football and eat turkey."

"Right," Lewa said. *Just like millions.*

"But that's not my favorite part," he said with a shy grin as if hesitant to share.

"What is?" she urged him.

"It's the leftovers. My mom always buys two huge turkeys 'cause we have a lot of guests, but we still end up with a lot of leftover turkey. The real fun is all the things she does with it."

Lewa stepped closer intrigued. "Like what?"

He brushed his hair back and thought for a moment. 'Turkey sandwiches, turkey pie, turkey enchiladas. You can do a lot."

He was right. She could do a lot. She was thinking of the turkey as something whole that couldn't be altered, but who said she had to bake it like everyone else? She could treat it like the basis of 'anything,' making her options limitless. "Thank you," she said grabbing a big baking pan then pushing her cart into the main aisle. 'Have a great Thanksgiving."

"You too."

Before going home, Lewa stopped at the international market and grabbed a packet of melon seeds and chili pepper then went home and baked the turkey--following a recipe she'd found--while she chopped a bowl full of miniature tomatoes and onions. She couldn't wait to show her family her new tradition.

THAT THANKSGIVING, Lewa boldly set her turkey dish on the table among the red jollof rice and yellow curried trout.

"What is this?" her mother asked as Lewa took the foil off.

Lewa looked at her mother with love, seeing the unease in her eyes. It would be another year before her sister gave birth to a boy and three years after that before Lewa walked down the aisle to an American man her family accepted with some hesitation, but none of those things--her sister's childless state or her unmarried one-- mattered to her that day. She finally knew who she was and what Thanksgiving meant to her. She was thankful for the freedom to be a her own person--to be unique and different without shame. Now she had her own special dish that would add to the season of traditions.

"It's meat pies," Aunty Elizabeth said recognizing a familiar staple.

"It's turkey pies," Lewa corrected. "Spiced with chili peppers and I added some other ingredients."

"They look good," her father said.

"I bet they'll be delicious," Stillman added.

"You'll make a good wife," her grandmother said.

But this time Lewa didn't mind the mention of her single state. She looked at her sister and Stillman, with no envy. The man for her was out there, somewhere. And if he wasn't, she was okay with that too. She'd gotten her turkey for Thanksgiving and hopefully started a new tradition. One that suited her just fine.

A CUP OF CHEER

A CUP OF CHEER

"No, no, no! I won't do it even for you."

"It's the holidays, Alyson. The least we can do as neighbors is spread good cheer."

"So you want me to give my delicious spiced cider to Scrooge next door?"

Of course his real name isn't Scrooge. It's Gareth LeBlanc owner of the second hand bookstore (creatively called Second Hand Books). Although the way he fussed over the books you'd think they were antiques instead of smelly old paperbacks and well worn hardbacks. I've only spoken to him a few times (when I wave 'hello', he just nods) and I can honestly say that I've only heard five sentences come out of his mouth. The only thing me or anyone else knows, was posted in a small write up in the weekly Community News: He was born in Dominica, the son of an English father and Dominican mother, and has travelled extensively.

When he first moved in, I sent him a box of cookies to welcome him to the neighborhood. I knew that he lived in the apartment above his shop, as I did, and I'd hoped to be as friendly with him as I had been with the previous residents—two elderly sisters from Trinidad who said my coconut cookies were divine. He didn't say they were divine, he didn't even say they were nice. He just returned an empty tin with a sticky note that said 'Thanks'. That's it, nothing more...just 'Thanks'.

It took me weeks before I could stomach the thought of stopping by his shop. I finally decided to visit in order to see the type of cookbooks he had. I have to give him credit, he had a pretty good selection. So every few weeks I'd stop by and buy a few. I was buying two when I noticed this beautifully bound book from the early twentieth century called *Amelia Armand's Complete Book of Spices*. It was encased in the curio behind his head. I was certain it would be expensive, but I was willing to pay the price.

I am a culinary historian and when I'm not in my store selling traditional and rustic crafts and recipe books, I recreate authentic dishes for functions at the Historical Society. A book like that would have been perfect for my collection.

"How much is that book behind you?" I asked after purchasing several items. He adjusted the rim of his baseball cap. He always wore a baseball cap (perhaps he was going bald) and a tie that never matched his shirt (and color blind?)-- orange against a tan shirt.

He didn't even turn around to see what I was referring to. "It's not for sale," he said in a cutting deep voice that could cause one to have goose bumps, if one liked the resonant sound of low baritones. I haven't stepped foot in that bookstore since. I'd rather drop my money in a sewer than fatten his bank account again.

"Since you're so desperate to spread holiday cheer why don't you do it?" I asked Cora.

"Because I didn't make the cider and it is better coming from you. You have that cheery, friendly aura about you."

"You mean jolly, don't you?"

She made a face, but wisely didn't reply. I'm not fat, but I'm not slim either. Not like Cora who has a nice slender build which she further accentuated by wearing tight suede trousers, a pink cashmere blouse and black boots with heels that could cause the sidewalk to crack. But I didn't envy her, I had inherited my stout full-figure like all the women in my family and was curvy in all the right places. My mother who had been born in Venezuela, of Trinidadian parents and Barbadian grand-parents had made sure, while I was growing up, that I would be proud of my figure. I preferred my loose fitting cotton tops and trousers and comfortable walking shoes. Customers said I made them feel at home and that feeling was always good for business.

"Besides, it's slick and icy outside," she complained. "You wouldn't want me to trip, would you?" She wiggled her high heeled boot.

"It would serve you right."

"But what would you do without me?"

I scowled. She was right; her business acumen had helped turn my small shop into an international destina-tion. I was getting mail orders from as far away as Dubai.

"He's not married, you know."

I rolled my eyes. "Yes, I heard Dracula is single too."

She sent me a look; I ignored her. Ever since I hired her as my assistant five years ago she's been trying to match me up. It's not that I don't like men. I do. Just not modern men. You know: the modern man who won't hold the door open for you, but instead will let it slam in your face; the modern man who expects you to pay for dinner while he pays for dessert; the modern man who thinks the question "Would you like to come inside?" means *you*.

I wanted something more. I wanted romance. Grand gestures like a carriage ride on a snowy day, or holding out my chair and remembering to walk on the outside of the pavement so that passing cars wouldn't splash me. Or even calling me by my name instead of 'honey' or babe' or confusing me for another woman (a long story). But I'd given up on romance years ago. Modern men didn't do grand gestures. They didn't even do small ones.

"Look, it's starting to snow," Cora said, glancing out the shop window. "How can you not be friendly at a time like this when everything looks white and fresh?" She shoved the thermos filled with hot cinnamon-nutmeg cider into my chest. "Go on and spread some holiday cheer."

"He'll probably bite my head off again," I mumbled slipping into my coat and hat.

"He's just a man, Alyson. Not the big bad wolf."

I made a face and wrapped a scarf around my neck.

THE WIND nearly knocked me back into the shop. A freezing blast stung my cheeks while a stream of cold tears fell from my eyes. *He's not worth this.* I turned around ready to go back in my store. Cora blocked the doorway and mouthed 'Go.' I briefly wondered how many homicides occurred during the holiday season then spun around and hurried next door.

The bell chimed above my head as I entered the shop. It was quiet with only a few customers rummaging through books on the shelves. I stomped my snow-covered boots on the rug and glanced towards the counter, which was conveniently empty. Perhaps he was out back somewhere polishing one of his beloved books. I could leave the cider on his desk with the added benefit of not having to see him. Great! I smiled in triumph, took one of his business cards and scribbled 'Happy Holidays' on the back.

Once finished I looked up and saw it: The book. I glanced side to side to make sure no one was watching then I lifted myself on the counter, leaned closer and squinted, hoping I could tell whether the book was really old or just an imitation. By looking at the paper texture and type it looked like the real thing. My mind raced with all the possible recipes hidden inside.

"It's not for sale."

I fell back and stumbled before regaining my footing. I stared at him. Or rather at his chest, since that was the first thing I saw. Today he wore a red shirt and green tie-- at least he looked festive. Although I doubt that was his intention, he didn't seem the festive sort. I finally raised my gaze to his face. As usual he wore his baseball cap low, shading his eyes. I was glad since I didn't care to read their expression. "You know I could offer you a lot of money..."

"It's still not for sale," he repeated in that same deep baritone.

"Then why do you have it there?"

"Because I like it there." He abruptly turned and went behind the counter. "But you're right, I should make things clear." He quickly wrote a sign that said 'Display Only' then taped it up. He then turned to me. "Better?"

I frowned, trying my best to look confused. "Does that mean it's not for sale?"

He blinked looking bored. "Did you want something?"

I didn't think he would have appreciated hot spiced cider over his head so I shoved the thermos into his chest, which was surprisingly harder than I thought it would be. Weren't dusty bookworms supposed to be a little soft around the middle? "This is for you."

He frowned and looked down at the thermos. "What is it?"

"It's poison."

He glanced up quickly. His surprise gave me a chance to look at his eyes, which were big, brown and oddly innocent.

No one with eyes like those could be all bad. "I was hoping to kill you off so I could steal the book."

The corner of his mouth kicked up as he twisted the lid and took a sniff. "Smells like hot cider."

"Spiced cinnamon-nutmeg cider if you want to be specific."

He poured himself a cup then took a sip, nodded as though in approval then looked at me with a playful glare that said a lot more. "It's still not for sale."

I shrugged, feigning defeat. "I know." I took a step back, suddenly feeling both restless and giddy at the same time. I knew it was time to leave. "Well, Happy Holidays." I turned and left before he could say anything more.

HE RETURNED the thermos the next day, or rather had it delivered. I had been working on our website when Cora came into the office. She held the thermos against her and said in a loud stage whisper. "It's from him."

"Him who?"

"Scrooge."

I pretended not to care, though I felt my face grow warm. "So? Set it in the kitchen."

She waved a piece of paper. "He sent you a note."

I took the envelope (Cora said I snatched it, but she tends to be dramatic). It was real parchment paper with my name scribbled across in his broad handwriting. For a moment I pictured him sitting at an old oak desk under a low hanging lamp, while a stripped cat sat on his shoulder, lazily waving its tail (Gareth didn't have a cat, but I liked the image). I could hear the smooth movement as his pen glided across the paper. Once he was finished, he carefully folded the note and placed it inside the envelope then slowly licked and sealed it closed. I brought the envelope to my nose. Did his scent cling to it or was it just my imagination?

Cora's voice cut into my daydream. "Aren't you going to open it?"

I blinked, shocked out of my fantasy, then ripped open the letter.

Dear Ms. Haywood:

There are few things in life that can be described as perfect: A starry sky, a new dawn and your spiced cinnamon-nutmeg cider. May I request another? Bring it by tomorrow. I will pay accordingly.

Sincerely,

Gareth LeBlanc

"What does it say?" Cora asked trying to peer over my shoulder. I handed her the note. She read it and frowned. "Well it certainly isn't poetry. Dear Ms. Haywood? It sounds so cold and formal. So what are you going to do?"

I wasn't sure, but I planned to think of something.

THE FOLLOWING DAY BROUGHT SUNSHINE, the sound of birds chirping, the distant ring of a Salvation Army Santa, and the steady drip of snow melting on the rooftop. I took my basket and headed next door. The sign on the door said 'Closed' and I was about to ring the bell when I looked through the store's glass front door and saw Gareth wearing a faded brown corduroy jacket and baseball cap talking to a woman in a long white cashmere coat. It didn't look like a happy conversation. I started to turn when the woman raced out the door in tears. Gareth followed, but didn't call out her name or tell her to stop. He just watched her go. It was obviously a lover's quarrel and not something I wanted to be a part of. I took two quick steps back hoping I could escape before he saw me.

"I hate the holidays," he mumbled then turned before I was a safe distance away. He stared at me surprised. "What do you want?"

I took another quick step back towards the freedom and safety of my store. "Nothing. I just--"

He held open the door. "Come on in."

I swallowed, wondering if I should refuse him, but decided to take the risk and go inside suddenly aware that it was the first time I'd ever been alone with him.

"I could come back another time."

He shook his head. "Doesn't matter. I shouldn't even be here." He gestured to the books around him. "All of this was my brother's idea. I was going to help him. He was the one with the pleasing personality and charm. He was going to be the one upfront dealing with the customers and I'd be in the back handling the accounting and other mundane business. He was so happy when he found this building and we signed the lease." Gareth angrily adjusted his cap. "After he died I should have just let everything go, but I couldn't. I wanted to fulfill this dream for him, but I'm all wrong. I'm not good with people--I prefer eReaders and computers and computer games. But the strange thing is that business is booming but Jani wants me to leave."

"Jani?"

"My ex-girlfriend, she's the one who just left. She wants me to give it up and return to my old job, but I can't." He stared at me and shook his head amazed. "I don't know why I'm telling you all this."

I smiled. "I'm easy to talk to."

He didn't return my smile, but his face softened. "You would have liked Rupert."

"His brother's not too bad either."

Gareth's gaze fell and I winced, knowing that's probably not something he wanted to hear. Now was not the time to flirt.

"The holidays can be hard for anyone," I said hoping to cover my gaffe and find a way to comfort him. "Especially when you've lost someone you care about, but I'm sure he'd want you to be happy."

Gareth let out a tired sigh. "He would and I'm letting him down. I mean what right do I have to be happy living his dream?"

"People don't own dreams and from what you've told me, it was a dream you had together. I bet you his spirit is here with you cheering you on."

Gareth sent me a long look I couldn't read. I licked my lip wondering if he was going to tell me to leave or mind my own business. Instead he spun around, said "Give me a minute" then disappeared upstairs.

I didn't move. I thought about leaving, but I was too curious to do so. I thought about his brother. I thought about how lonely it must be for Gareth to be here in this empty shop.

"Okay, come up," he called from above.

I hesitated then walked up the stairs to the main

landing then into a nice living area. The heat of a crackling fire met me first, followed by the sounds of carols drifting from the radio. A tiny Christmas tree sat on the windowsill with a crooked star on top. I straightened it, crooked things annoy me.

"I thought you hated Christmas," I called out to him.

"I changed my mind," he said from another room. "Take a seat."

"No, I have something to show you first."

"More cider?"

"No. I'm going to show you how to make your own."

He came out of the other room and stared at me surprised. I stared back equally stunned. He wasn't wearing his hat. Although everything else was the same —he wore a dreadful checkered maroon tie with a striped shirt—I felt as though I'd met him half dressed, exposed. I'd uncovered his secret. He wasn't going bald, he had cropped black hair, and the most expressive deep brown eyes I'd ever seen. Every emotion he felt flashed in them; I could see they were his most vulnerable feature. And something in their expression seemed to ignite something inside me. Something I'd ignored for a long time. I'd buried myself in history and the past so that I wouldn't be vulnerable in the present, but at that moment Gareth had shown me that people hadn't changed that much. Their hopes, fears and dreams remained the same.

His eyes changed from surprised to weariness. "You're going to teach me?"

"Yes."

He flashed one of his odd little half smiles then disappeared into the room again, he reappeared with his base-ball cap.

I took it off. "You look better without it."

He put it back on. "It brings me luck."

"You don't need luck."

He grabbed my hand before I could take it off. "How about courage then? It's a crutch, but it works for me. Superman has his cape, Wolverine has his claws and I have my cap, okay?"

"Fine," I said, though I wondered how I could convince him otherwise. He really did have very nice eyes.

Gareth showed me the kitchen and we both went inside. Making cinnamon-nutmeg cider only takes ten minutes. Somehow I made it last an hour; neither of us noticed the time. As the cider simmered on the stove the smell of cloves, nutmeg, apples, cinnamon, and sweet brown sugar permeated the air.

When the cider was done we sat in his alcove that looked down into the quiet bookshop and drank in peaceful silence.

"Books make sorry companions after awhile," he finally said.

Both pain and resignation seeped behind his simple words. "History can lose its appeal too," I said.

We slipped into silence again then he abruptly stood, picked up a book from off the shelf and handed it to me.

I stared at him stunned. "*Amelia Armand's Complete Book of Spices*? You can't *give* this to me."

He took a sip of his cider and sent me a full grin. "I'm

not. It's still not for sale." He tipped his hat back a bit. "But you can come by and use it anytime."

I set the book down--at that moment I didn't care what was inside—instead I took his cap off and placed it on my head. It was a bold move to make, but I was a modern woman and decided to take the risk.

And he being a modern man...well let's just say I didn't open *Amelia Armand's Complete Book of Spices* until late New Years and I didn't mind a bit.

NEW YEAR'S SURPRISE

NEW YEAR'S SURPRISE

Divorce. Millions of people did it, but that didn't stop Pam Rubin from feeling alone. The man she'd thought she'd spend the rest of her life with would no longer be part of it. She knew it was the right decision. They'd been separated six months now, but they'd been emotionally apart longer than that. Living in the same house but living separate lives. She still didn't know where things had gone wrong. When had they stopped loving each other? When had simple disagreements become a war?

But she didn't want to think about that now. She had come to her sister's New Years Eve party, instead of staying home with her dog and watching the ball drop on TV, to cast aside the loneliness that seemed to stick to her skin like masking tape. No, tonight was a promise of new things and a new future. Pam stood with a glass in her hand, a fake look of joy on her face, feeling out of step with all the happy couples that surrounded her. It was strange how as her marriage crumbled that's all she started to see: happy newlyweds, happy parents with their children, happy older couples celebrating decades together. She and Jerrod had only made five years and there had been no children, but not for lack of trying.

Pam leaned against the balcony railing. The stars shone bright above her. She preferred looking at them instead of all the ruby earrings and emerald necklaces that graced the ladies inside the house. The dazzling gold wedding bands and diamond engagement rings seemed to sparkle under the lights, catching her eye where ever she turned. She glanced down at her now bare hand her loneliness making her feel invisible.

"There you are!" her sister, Darlene, said coming up to her, wearing a slinky sequence dress her own wedding ring twinkling under the Japanese lanterns that decorated the balcony. She was four years older with bouncing black curls and light brown eyes. She was usually considered the prettier of the two sisters because of her vivacious personality and engaging smile that some said was as sweet as grata cake. "I was looking all over for you! What are you doing standing out here by yourself? You're a single woman now, you should be living it up."

Pam shook her head, a strand of hair falling from her French twist. She narrowed her dark brown eyes. "I'm not single yet."

"You will be. You might as well start the New Year with a new man. Out with the old and in with the new."

Pam knew her sister didn't understand how raw she still felt. She didn't want a new man when she still couldn't understand how she'd lost the old one. "I'm not ready yet."

"It's been six months. Admit that it's over between you. You told me how happy you've been with him away. It may feel awkward, but it's time to get into the dating pool again."

"I don't know how to swim," Pam said in a dry attempt at humor.

"Just stay in the shallow end. Lucky for you your big sister is here to help. I have someone who is perfect for you."

Pam inwardly groaned. "I've given up on men."

Darlene opened her mouth then closed it then opened it again and said in a low, cautious tone. "So you're into women now?"

Pam laughed. "I'm not into anyone now. I am just through with relationships. I'm happier by myself."

Darlene visibly relaxed and rested a hand on her sister's shoulder her voice eager. "You're going to like him. He--"

"I don't care."

"You will care when you meet him. His parents are from Barbados and he has a doctorate in..." She frowned. "I forgot," she said with a careless wave of her hand. "But he's smart and I know that you like that in a man."

Pam sent her sister a look. He sounded just like her soon-to-be-ex. "I didn't come here to meet anybody."

Her sister clasped her hands together as if ready to beg. "If you'll just meet him, I will leave you alone. I promise. I really want you to meet him."

Pam set her wine glass down. It wasn't like her sister to be so insistent. Since she'd agreed to come to the party she might as well try to be sociable. "Okay. Let me go freshen up."

"Yes," Darlene said as Pam turned to leave. "Don't forget to add more lipstick, take the shine off your nose and for goodness sake consider letting your hair down."

PAM STARED at her reflection in the bathroom mirror, feeling as though she was staring at a stranger. Who was that woman with hollow eyes and pinched lips? When was the last time she'd smiled? She shouldn't have come. She didn't want to meet anyone. She wasn't ready to. She knew her sister meant well but that didn't make her feel better. She had to leave. She would grab her coat and go. Satisfied with her plan, Pam left the bathroom and headed for the room where all the coats were piled up on a bed. She was halfway down the hall ready to go upstairs when she saw her sister standing next to a man. He looked very genial and attractive, but she didn't want to meet him. She prayed her sister didn't turn and see her. She wanted to escape. Pam frantically glanced around then darted into the first door she saw: The closet. She knew it was cowardly but she didn't care.

The closet had a familiar pleasant smell of lemon and spice, relaxing her a bit. She leaned against the wall, letting out a startled screech when it moved.

"Shh, you'll give us away," a deep voice said.

"What are you doing in here?" she demanded in a loud whisper.

"I wanted to be alone."

"Then why did you come to a party?"

"I was invited," he said. "But now I'm not sure that was a good idea."

"Then why don't you go home?" Pam asked annoyed by the tremor in her voice. She was used to being calm in any situation but this man had unnerved her.

"Because I just got here."

"You're being ridiculous."

"I could say the same about you," he said with laughter in his voice.

He was right. His reasons for hiding were eerily similar to hers. She should follow her own advice and just leave. "I'm sorry," she said then became quiet when she heard people passing by. "You just scared the living daylights out of me. I'm hiding from my sister." Pam folded her arms then looked up at the figure next to her. She was unable to see his face clearly except for some light that seeped through the slits in the closet door. It highlighted a forehead, nose and mouth. She took several deep breaths and soon her heartbeat returned to normal. She should be panicked and waited for anxiety to seize her, but oddly it didn't. After the initial shock of surprise she felt strangely resigned by the situation. At least she knew where the lemon and spice scent came from. Every time he moved the scent seemed to embrace her and reminded her of happier times.

"So why are you hiding from your sister?" he asked.

Pam briefly shut her eyes. She hadn't expected the question. She didn't want him to care. Wasn't sure she could trust him. But somehow the darkness was a comfort. What was it about the dark that made sharing seem safe? That made two people feel intimate? She didn't think too much about it. She was relieved to have the chance to speak to a man she'd never speak to again.

"She wants to fix me up with a man."

"Don't you like men?"

"I'm not very lucky with them."

"I don't believe that."

She sniffed. He would say that and eight years ago she would have believed him. She'd met her soon-to-be-ex at a party like this. But she'd been a different woman then. A woman with a promising future and bright ideas. She'd worn a blue velvet dress and spinning gold earrings. She'd just escaped the attention of two graduate students who'd bored her with their pretentiousness when a tall man stepped into her path and said, "A professor or a teacher?"

She looked at him startled. "What?"

He held out his arms to the side. "Do I look like a professor or a teacher?"

Pam surveyed his clothes and shook her head puzzled. He didn't look like either. He looked like a corporate raider. He wore all black, which only emphasized a large intimidating build. He had a carefully trimmed goatee, his black hair shone low, skin like molasses, feather-like long lashes and piercing brown eyes. "Does it matter?" she asked.

He let out a sigh. "Yes, I've got a job interview in a week and I really need to make the right impression. I've already had ten others with no results."

"Well, first you're too on the point?"

He frowned. "On the point?"

"Yes," she said with a light laugh. "I don't even know your name."

He held out his hand Jerrod Fuller."

"I'm Pam Rubin and I don't think you look like a teacher or professor. Anyone looking at you would see an ambitious young man who would take over their job one day."

He raised a dark eyebrow. "I'm ambitious."

"You don't have to wear it like a banner. You can go for business casual. Also focus on the needs of the school. How you'll be a value to them."

Jerrod nodded. "I can do that. Are you free tomorrow?"

Pam paused. "For what?"

"For dinner. I'd like to get more of your advice."

"But I don't have much to say," Pam stuttered feeling her face grow warm.

A sly grin touched the corner of his mouth. "I'm sure you do and I'm prepared to listen to every word."

And he did. He just let her talk and his dark eyes watched her as if she were the most fascinating and beautiful woman in the world. And she in turn helped him soften his look so that he didn't appear so intimidating. Although he looked like the kind of man who'd likely have gotten into college on a sports scholarship he'd actually gotten a scholarship in science, played tennis and had a passion for abstract art. A week later he aced his interview. A week after that he was hired and a month later they were inseparable. Their first New Years Eve together had been simple and beautiful. A quiet time at home with a bottle of champagne and a ring. He'd told her he wanted to spend every New Year with her and asked her to marry him. And she'd said yes. It had all seemed so perfect but she hadn't known that something would destroy that peace. That it had a name.

Fear. How come no one ever talked about how fear can enter a marriage? How it can erode trust and communication? How it can slowly eat away at what one has struggled to build? Pam still remembered her mother's sneer on the day of the rehearsal dinner. "He's just a teacher. He's got no money. There's no need to marry the bastard."

Pam gritted her teeth. "He's not a bastard."

"One day you'll think so."

"No, I won't. I love him."

"That will change."

Had it? Had it changed? The butterflies had gone and familiarity had taken away the rush of romantic surprise and the high of falling in love. But the sun was also familiar, however she never grew tired of its dancing rays. It had been the same with Jerrod except, unlike the sun, she'd started to worry that he wouldn't always be there. And one day she'd been right. She hadn't wanted to be her mother, but she'd taken her mother's bitterness and fear into the marriage. Their six months apart had taught her a lot about herself.

She used to watch Jerrod at a party with admiration so glad that he was hers. She didn't even know when her casual glances turned to suspicion. When she'd watch him with a woman with careful surveillance as though a police officer on the trail of a suspect. She would watch how he tilted his head, his eyes, his smile. She'd watch the woman too. Notice how she touched him, if it was a hand to his shoulder or his sleeve and she'd wondered what the gesture meant. She never confronted him because she knew what he would say. Her father had said the same. She just let her suspicions grow and her fears mingled with them until there was a wall around her heart. She knew he felt it too, but they never talked about it. Soon they never talked about anything not pay cuts, tight schedules or family illnesses and after their last attempt at having a child she knew there was nothing else to keep them together.

Pam sighed feeling the weight of her loss. She'd loved him. She'd thought he'd loved her. Where had it gone wrong? She angrily brushed away a clothes hanger, wishing she'd brought a glass of wine in the closet with her.

"I'm sure he has no problems with the ladies," Pam said sourly, wanting to take the focus off of her. "He never did."

"You never know."

She nodded. "You're right. I don't. I stopped knowing very much about him after awhile. Somehow we just stopped talking."

"Did you ever try to talk?"

"Yes, but it soon became too painful, especially when we couldn't have kids. I know how much he wants to be a father."

She heard him rub his hands together. "I doubt that's the only reason he married you."

"Well it seemed that's where everything fell apart."

"I bet there were other things. I mean my wife only

cared about starting a family, but for me it was too stressful."

"You don't want kids?" she asked more sharply than she wanted to. "I mean it's okay if you don't," she added more softly not wanting him to stop talking.

"I did--do, but at the time my father was dying and I couldn't focus on anything else."

His words made her heart constrict with sorrow. "I'm sorry about your father."

He sighed. "He loved my wife. I'm glad he didn't see my marriage end."

"Did you love your wife?"

"Still do."

Her voice cracked with surprise and suspicion. "Really?"

"Yes, everyone keeps telling me to move on and I know I should, but something is holding me back and I think that's it."

"Sometimes our hearts mislead us."

He shook his head. "Not often, especially not mine."

Pam fell silent unable to believe his words. They sounded genuine, but if he really loved his wife why hadn't he fought to keep his marriage? She rubbed her forehead, wishing she could gather her warring thoughts, then let her hand fall. "If you could do it all again, what would you do?"

He was silent a long moment then said, "Apologize for not admitting how unhappy I was. I would have been more honest. You?"

"Same. I would have given him more space. I wanted him to talk to me and I think that just pushed him further away. I wanted him to turn to me. But he turned to someone else instead."

"Are you sure about that?"

"Positive."

"How?"

Pam shrugged feeling the wall around her heart starting to rebuild. "The usual," she said trying to sound casual although the memory of his deception pierced her. "Secret phone calls. Cryptic notes. Strange perfume on his clothes." She'd been taught by her twice divorced mother that if you didn't have a man's attention someone else did. Her father hadn't been true to any of his five wives. Now that he was older he was slowing down so wife number six may be lucky. Women found Jerrod attractive and he never had trouble getting noticed. She was attractive too, but she knew that wasn't enough to keep a man. Her mother had been beautiful and kept the house running while also working and that still hadn't made her father faithful. Without kids Pam couldn't think of anything to get Jerrod to stay.

"Did you tell him?"

"No," Pam said quickly. "I didn't want to know the details. I failed him. I didn't want to know about the woman who hadn't. I'd once been the most important woman in his life and then it ended. When a man cheats it's over."

"So if he'd told you why he cheated you wouldn't have forgiven him?"

"Sure I'd forgive him, but I couldn't trust him. If he's unhappy he deserves to leave. It's just a symptom. I'm sure he's happy with whoever he's with now."

"Trust is important."

"Yes."

"My wife never trusted me."

Pam paused surprised by his statement. She drummed her fingers against her thigh. "Did you give her a reason not to?"

"No. I could never do or say enough to make her believe in me. At first she did. She made me feel like the greatest man on the planet and then, after we married, that changed. I gave her gifts. I told her how much I loved her, but if I came home late or she saw me with a female colleague she'd assume the worse."

Pam released a tired sigh feeling suddenly worn. "I guess that's unfair."

"Yes. You can't have a relationship without trust."

"Hmm."

"But I lied. I did give my wife a reason not to trust me."

"I knew it," Pam said satisfied that he was just as she'd suspected him to be: A typical male. "What was it?"

"I kept a secret from her."

She bit her lip her heart picking up pace. "What?"

"After my father died I started thinking about my own morality. It can hit a man hard sometimes. I went to get checked and discovered I was genetically disposed to have the same condition that killed my father. I started to do lots of tests and even started therapy to deal with my fear."

"Why didn't you tell m--her? Why keep that a secret?"

"Because by that time she was so focused on having a

family and not succeeding and I didn't want to feel as if I'd failed her on something else."

"But she would have been there for you. I know she didn't marry you just so that you could be a father."

"It's broken up marriages before."

"But if you'd talked..." Pam let her words trail off. Obviously he hadn't trusted her.

He shifted, the sleeve of his shirt brushing hers, the lemon and spice sense embracing her again. "Too bad you never talked about it."

"Yes."

"I guess we both failed," he said.

Pam hugged herself, feeling the wall around her heart crumbling but terrified of being vulnerable again as she let hope seep in. "Think there's any way to fix it?"

"Maybe by remembering the good times. Where there any?"

Pam smiled. "Yes."

"Tell me."

"I used to love when he'd sing off key in the shower. He has a really good voice and knew his singing would always make me laugh and it did. He also used to have this strange way of knowing who was calling without looking at the caller ID. He'd be in the living room reading and the phone would ring and he'd say "Pick up it's your mother" or "Forget it, it's my sister." And more often than not he was right. I used to tease him that he was psychic. We loved going to concerts. Indoor , outdoor, bands, symphonies. Anything. He could always make the outing an adventure because he knew how to move in a crowd. In the early days I loved to listen to him talk about his students and he supported me while I got my Masters. Even when I felt like giving up he always believed in me."

"Sounds like good times."

Pam felt her heart lift. "They were." She hesitated then asked, "How about you?"

"My wife used to put lollipops in my briefcase with a note that said 'Have a sweet day.' She'd also coordinate the closet by color, matching shirts with ties, belts with pants, socks with shoes."

Pam groaned. "She sounds controlling."

He shook his head and laughed. "I liked it. I didn't have to think hard. If I grabbed a shirt I could see what tie could go with it. It made my morning easier and made me feel that she cared about me."

"She still doesn't sound like much fun."

"Maybe to some. I know with you having a husband who likes to go out and mingle and have different adventures you wouldn't understand how important it can be to have a place that's organized. Someone who is settled and grounded. I grew up around a lot of chaos and my wife helped me learn to live a different way. Just being with her was fun. We'd sit together and just talk or watch TV or play a video game, or tell corny jokes. I miss that. I miss her."

Pam blinked back tears. "I miss him too, but are memories really enough? I was so afraid of losing him that I pushed him away. I don't think I can fix that." It was too much. The man, the memories. Suddenly instead of feeling like a confessional the closet felt like a tomb. She couldn't breathe. She grabbed the door and opened it desperate to escape.

He grabbed her arm. "Pam wait."

She shook her head. "When I first heard your voice I nearly ran out."

"I'm glad you didn't," he said in a velvet whisper, tenderly turning her to face him.

She squeezed her eyes shut. She couldn't look at him. It had been so intimate in the closet and had felt safe, but now she felt exposed. She didn't want to look at him, but she knew she had to. She gathered her courage and faced him: The tall good looking man with skin like molasses and featherlike lashes who'd helped her sort through her mixed feelings. The man who had once asked her if he looked like a teacher or professor. The man who'd asked her to marry him on New Years' Eve.

"I want you back," Jerrod said.

"Why?" Pam said in a broken voice.

"I'm sorry I pulled away from you and kept secrets. I know it was wrong, but I want a second chance."

"But why?"

"I told. I love you."

"But I pushed you away with my suspicions and--"

"You made a mistake and I did too. That makes us human. And one thing I've learned about being human is that we can break, but we can also heal." His gaze fell. "When your sister invited me I wasn't going to come. I was angry, but somehow she convinced me." His gaze met and held hers. "I'm glad I did."

"But you ended up in the closet."

A sheepish grin touched his lips. "I know. When I

saw you I couldn't face you so I hid. And the next thing I knew you were in here too."

"Hiding from my sister." Pam took his large hand and cradled it in hers. "I guess it's time we both stopped hiding."

"Yes."

She lightly brushed her thumb over the back of his hand. "My sister thought I should start the upcoming year with a new man."

Jerrod pulled her into the circle of his arms and he looked down at her as if she were the most fascinating and beautiful woman he knew. "I am a new man and I'm all yours, if you want me."

Pam cupped his face in her hands and kissed him. "I love you," she whispered against his lips, wanting him to know that she still thought he was the greatest man in the world. She gave her heart to him with complete trust, casting all fear away.

His lips met hers with a tender silent vow and at that moment their wounds began to heal. Neither noticed when the clock struck twelve.

Darlene saw them and raised a glass relieved that her plan had worked. "Happy New Year you two. May it be filled with many more wonderful surprises."

A MOTHER'S DAY WISH

"We don't need you. We have a lawn service to take care of things," Beth Armstrong said looking at the lanky fifteen year old who'd asked to mow her lawn. She was surprised he'd even offered. He was a Bailey after all and everyone knew the Baileys were a lazy bunch. The only effort his father extended was to find a woman and get his pants down or open a bottle and fill his belly with liquor. People knew better than to hire him because he'd never show up, but would always come up with an excuse as to why. Just like his father before him. Even his great-grandfather had a notorious reputation back in Trinidad. He'd been a man not to be trusted. Beth didn't expect young Cole Bailey to be much different. He was a good looking young man with dark lashes and brows, but the Bailey men always were.

She hardened her heart against the look of disappointment that dimmed Cole's light brown eyes and turned the corners of his mouth down. She couldn't bend. She wouldn't. People had been trying to help the Baileys for years and nothing ever worked. She gripped the door handle, stiffened her spine and let a slight, polite smile touch her lips. "I'm sorry. Goodbye and good day."

"Good day," Cole said not meaning a word. He forced a smile then turned. It didn't feel like a good day but that was all he'd been forced to hear. The Armstrong house had been his last stop. Nobody would hire him. He'd offered lawn care, window washing, spider web cleaning and painting, but he always got a polite 'good day' and a door in his face. He knew the people of Hamsford didn't want a Bailey inside their homes, but he'd hoped they'd at least let him help outside with the grunt work. Wasn't he good enough for that? None of the local shop owners would give him work, his father and grandfather's reputations always proceeded him. But he wasn't his father or grandfather.

Unfortunately, no one would give him the chance to prove it. And he needed a break. He needed to make money to help his family, especially his younger sisters who deserved more than what they were getting--a fridge that was usually empty and a cramped, dank apartment. His parents were already two months late on the rent. Cole knew the rent was really six months overdue, but his father had managed to bargain it down to two months since he was sleeping with the landlord's wife and she'd somehow persuaded her husband to lower what was owed. Cole didn't know how long the arrangement would last, since his father never stuck with anyone or anything long. He wanted to make sure he had enough money to take care of the family in case something went wrong, which it usually did.

Yes, his sisters deserved better. Just thinking of them made him smile. They were the only people in town who loved and looked up to him. They were so sweet and smart. He remembered when he'd gone to the church charity looking for clothes he'd picked up an old stain glass kit for his thirteen year old sister, Angela. She made amazing art with it, which he put up near the windows giving their gloomy place some beauty as it cast rainbows on the walls and floor. He wanted to get her some more tools and pay for a school trip to an art gallery in two months. Then there was his shy little sister, Grace, who needed braces. She was ten and her teeth were growing in crooked. Kids were already making fun of her and she had no friends.

Not that his parents noticed. His mother was always in a foul mood, angry that she'd ended up marrying a 'good for nothing Bailey' and getting 'good for nothing children.' His father was hardly around but nobody missed him anyway.

Cole slowly walked down the path that cut through the Armstrong's manicured lawn trying to think of another way to make money when he saw an older woman coming towards him carrying heavy bags. He rushed up to her. "Let me help you," he said half expecting her to refuse. People didn't let Baileys help them.

"Oh thank you," she said offering him a bright smile of relief. "I bought more than I should have."

Cole stopped and stared at her for a moment in amazement. She'd smiled at him. Not a fake distant smile, but a real genuine one. He'd never had that before. He took her bags even more eager to please her just to get her to smile at him again. She had a nice round face, sparkling eyes, warm brown skin and grey hair. If he had a grandmother he'd want one to be just like her. He helped her carry her bags to the door, wishing he could help her with something else.

"Thank you young man," she said taking her keys out of her handbag.

"My pleasure," he said liking the soft island lilt of her words.

"What's your name?"

Suddenly, the door swung open, cutting off his reply. "Mother," Beth said in an urgent rush. "Are you okay?"

"I'm perfectly fine," she said startled. "This young man--"

Beth snatched the bags from Cole and anxiously peered inside. "You'd better check to make sure everything is here. Baileys have sticky fingers."

The woman shot her daughter a glance of annoyance. "Of course everything is there. I didn't raise you to be facety like this."

Beth sent Cole a look of suspicion. "Why are you back here? I told you we can't use you."

"He was helping me."

Beth set the bags aside and pulled money from her purse. She held out a five dollar bill and waved it at him with impatience."Fine you can go now."

Cole took a step back, trying to take rein on his temper. He wanted to take the five dollars and ram it in her mouth. He could show her how much of a sticky fingered no good Bailey he could be. Instead he gripped his hands into fists. "I'm gone."

"Wait," the older woman said grabbing his sleeve. "What did you come for?"

"To mow the lawn," Beth said.

Her mother stared at her, raising her eyebrows. "Is this a puppet show? I ask him a question and you answer?"

"No, mother but--"

"Then keep your mouth shut 'til I ask you to open it again." She turned her attention to Cole. "Come inside. I want to talk to you." Before her daughter could protest the woman stepped past her and said, "Put the kettle on. I'm thirsty." She ignored the stunned silence that followed her request and headed for the kitchen.

Cole hesitated then followed. He'd never been inside such a fine house before. He gaped at the rose colored wallpaper and polished wooden floors. There wasn't a cockroach in sight. When he passed the family room he quickly peeked inside and saw Mr. Armstrong standing near the fireplace and his son, Grant, reading a book. He knew Grant from school, not personally, but from a distance and by reputation. Grant always had a crowd of admirers around him since he was a track star and talented musician. Cole was too in awe to notice the frown on Grant's face when he saw him. He hurried to the kitchen then halted at the sight of how large it was. His entire apartment could fit inside it.

"Sit down," the woman said getting some Jamaican bun and cheese out of the refrigerator. She set them on the table.

He sat, rubbing his hands together under the table. "Yes, Mother Armstrong."

"No," she said with a laugh. "I'm not an Armstrong. That's my daughter's married name. Just call me Ms. Hetty."

"Hey Bailey," a voice said behind him. He turned and saw Grant standing in the doorway, a look of annoyance on his face. "What are you doing here?"

Cole opened his mouth to reply, but Hetty beat him to it. "We're having a private conservation. You can talk to him later."

Grant scowled then stormed away.

"So you do lawn care?" Hetty asked.

"Yes ma'am," he said. He'd tried to join a landscaping crew but no one would hire him. However, he'd watched them work and picked up skills. He didn't have the equipment, but knew how they worked.

"What else can you do?"

Beth came into the kitchen and filled the kettle at the sink.

"Polish silver," he said.

She set the kettle on the stove and mumbled, "And steal it too."

Cole shifted in his seat, wanting to defend himself but knowing he couldn't.

"Go on," Hetty urged.

"I can clean spider webs."

Beth rested a hand on her hip. "You think I'd allow spiders to build webs in my house? My house is spotless."

"I didn't mean to offend."

"You might as well say you'd kill mice too."

"I can if you need me too."

Beth gasped. "You cheeky little--"

"Quiet, Beth," her mother interrupted.

She pointed at Cole. "Did you just hear what he said? He sits in my home and implies that we have mice!"

"Be quiet."

"But--"

Hetty turned to her daughter. "Have you forgotten that I'm still your mother? I said keep your mouth shut and I mean it. I can still box your ears and I'll make it your mouth if I have to." She turned back to Cole. "Go on."

He cleared his throat. "I'm good at fixing things."

"Anything in particular?"

"Anything you ask me to."

Hetty nodded. "Good I have a task for you. I have a lawn swing that needs to be fixed. Can you do that?"

"Yes."

"How much?" Cole gave her a price and she shook her head. "Too high."

Cole rubbed his hands and swallowed. He didn't want to lose her business, but he also didn't want to admit that he didn't even own a hammer or screwdriver. He needed money to buy tools. "I'll also paint the trim if you like."

"The price is still too high."

He lowered his gaze. *Think Bailey. You need this job.* He knew what his father would do. He'd try to sweet talk her, but he was no good at that. He liked to be honest. He sighed he hoped that wouldn't be a mistake. "I can lower the price if you'd allow me to use your tools."

Beth opened her mouth then quickly closed it, remembering her mother's threat.

"How much?" Hetty asked.

He gave her another price.

Hetty smiled and held out her hand. "Agreed. Come back tomorrow after ten."

Cole shook her hand, careful not to pump it too hard. He really wanted to give her a big hug. He'd made her smile and now had a job. He grinned back. "I will. Good day," he said, meaning every word.

AT DINNER BETH bristled with outrage. "You won't believe what Mother did today. She hired a Bailey."

Arthur Armstrong looked at his mother-in-law, who was calmly eating her dinner, then at the pinched face of his wife. His three sons waited to see how he would handle the situation. He chose to proceed with caution. "To do what?"

"Does it matter?"

"I'm curious."

"Fix the lawn swing."

"Why didn't you say so, Mother? I could have gotten it fixed for you."

Hetty did not raise her gaze from the curried trout and creamy scalloped potatoes on her plate. "On three occasions I asked but no one listened. I was tired of waiting."

"Mother," he said in a soft patronizing tone. "You're

new to this place so you don't know the people. Some of them you just can't trust."

"Exactly," Beth said. "The Bailey men are lazy, worthless men. What will people think? You don't know what you've done."

"I know exactly what I've done. I gave a young man a chance," Hetty said.

"But he's a--"

"He's not his father. Let him prove himself."

Grant touched her shoulder. "I'll fix it for you, Gran."

Hetty repressed a shudder. It wasn't good to not like one's own flesh and blood but she didn't take to her grandson. She found him to be as slick as palm oil. After her husband's death she'd looked forward to moving in with her daughter's family, but the move hadn't been as peaceful as she'd hoped. Her daughter was constantly correcting her, her son-in-law ignored her and her grandchildren barely noticed her. She'd carried heavy shopping bags before without anyone caring. To everyone she was just an invisible old woman. That young Bailey boy had been the first to take any notice. To really make her feel as if she mattered, not to feel as if she were just a burden or obligation. She had plenty of money, because she and her husband had been savvy with their finances, and could go to a residential facility, but she didn't want to be around just old people. But being around the younger generations wasn't much fun either. At times she considered moving to the cottage she and her husband still owned in New York and had used as a holiday house, but it would be lonely there.

"I've already hired Cole," Hetty said. "And I plan to keep my word."

"But--"

"I'm a grown woman and I've made up my mind. This has nothing to do with any of you."

THAT EVENING HETTY took out an old photograph and sat on her bed staring at the faded image. It was a picture of her cousin Lenny, a fine looking young man who'd been shot and killed in an armed robbery bust when the police mistook him for one of the assailants. She remembered returning to Trinidad to attend his funeral. She let her finger trail over his smiling happy face. No one had given him a chance. No one had taken the time to look past his poor grades and background to see what a hardworking young man he was. She remembered how he could make you smile when you wanted to cry and how he never felt sorry for himself. Cole somehow reminded her of him. Unlike Lenny, she would make sure he was given an opportunity to prove himself. But she knew helping Cole wasn't just for him, it was for her. She glanced around her crowded bedroom filled with stuff she could afford, but didn't need. It offered her no comfort. She was restless. She had done her childrearing and had worked most of her life. She'd waited all her life for these days of leisure, but she was bored. She wanted to do something. She wanted a reason to live. Cole had not only noticed her, he'd made her feel useful. He'd made her feel viable again.

COLE ARRIVED the next day at ten on the dot. Hetty sat in a lawn chair and watched him work. He was a good worker. Skinnier than he should be but strong. He told her about his sisters. They laughed together that Saturday like two kids getting to know each other and shared a lunch of spicy chicken patties and talked about their frustrations.

"No one will give me a chance," Cole said as they finished their meal.

"I did and I know others will too."

"I really want to thank you."

Hetty waved his thanks aside. "It's not a big issue. I'm glad you could help me and respect me." She sighed. "Sometimes my family treats me as if I were two years old."

"I wish I could take you home with me," Cole said. "I'd let you do whatever you wanted."

"Where do you live?"

Cole shook his head. "It's not good enough for you." He wondered if he'd ever have a place good enough for her to visit. Baileys had never owned anything. But he pushed the thought away and finished fixing her swing. Hetty giggled with delight when it was finished and immediately tried it out. She then gave him another task and soon he was a regular at the Armstrong house. To his surprise, word quickly spread and he was able to get other small jobs around town. But no job compared to working for Ms. Hetty, Cole thought as he dug up a patch of dirt she wanted to use as a herb garden. She was one of the most wonderful women he'd ever met: Smart and pretty and sweet and he loved her.

He'd given her a card for Mother's Day wishing he could spend every Mother's Day with her and treat her and his sisters to brunch like other families did. His mother hated Mother's Day and didn't like cards. She said they were just expensive pieces of paper unless there was money inside. But not Ms. Hetty. When Cole had given her his card--he'd wanted to get her perfume or flowers but a card was all he could afford--she'd given him one of her beaming smiles and held the card close as if he'd given her a treasure. Even though her family had treated her to buffet and gifts of scarves and jewelry she made him feel that his gift was just as important. And that night he wished he could always make her smile and imagined spending every holiday with her from New Year's Day to Christmas. He wished he could rescue her somehow. He hated to know she was unhappy living with her family. He knew how she felt, but he didn't know what he could do. He was close to raising enough money for Angela's school trip and with more jobs he could raise enough for Grace, but helping Ms. Hetty would take a miracle. At least he was glad that luck was finally on his side.

Grant watched Cole from his bedroom window with seething anger. Why was his grandmother paying attention to that dirty old Bailey? His friends were already ribbing him about it. Bailey was making him a laughing stock. He was the one who was supposed to shine. He was the track star and musician, but his grandmother barely took notice of him. What was so important about a stupid swing anyway? And why did she keep having to have him come back? Bailey almost acted like he belonged there, but he didn't. Hell, he could even sense his parents starting to like him and his two brothers had once asked Bailey to join them for a soccer game. He hated Cole Bailey. He should know his place.

That night Grant went into the garden and unscrewed a major hinge on the swing. He smiled as he imagined the havoc he'd just created. Now Bailey would get what he deserved.

HETTY LOVED to sit outside on late spring evenings. She was so happy that she now had a beautiful swing to sit in. Outside she felt close to Lenny and her husband and no longer thought of them with pain. Her heart had a new resident. Cole had filled her life with laughter and joy. She hoped to one day meet Cole's sisters since he talked so fondly about them. She sat on her swing and swayed back and forth then she heard a snap and the swing came crashing down. Shooting pain followed. She cried out as hot tears filled her eyes.

Beth rushed to her. "Mother!" She turned to her husband who'd followed close behind and said, "Call an ambulance."

Minutes later Hetty was taken to the hospital where they discovered she'd broken her hip. Infection quickly set in and for days Hetty was gravely ill, but to the relief of her family she pulled through.

Cole, however, soon found his world shattered. Word quickly spread about his poor workmanship and soon he was being called a 'no good Bailey' again and what little work he'd been able to get dried up.

"So typical," his mother said as he cleared up the fast food dinner he'd bought with money he'd saved. She sniffed in disgust. "You Bailey men always screw up a good thing."

"I know I fixed it right," Cole said, wishing there had been leftovers for tomorrow night's dinner. The greasy chicken meal was nothing like the baked plantain and jerk chicken Ms. Hetty had once treated him to, but it was still food.

His mother rested back in her chair, putting her feet on the table. Her boots added to the many scratches that were already there. "Then why did it break nearly killing the old woman?"

Cole swallowed feeling a little ill. "I don't know, but I didn't make a mistake. I tested it myself and I'm heavier than Ms. Hetty. I would never do anything to hurt her."

"Just take responsibility," Angela said. "Go to the hospital and ask for forgiveness."

He shook his head. "I can't face her."

"I thought she was your friend," his youngest sister, Grace, said.

Cole blinked back tears. She was and that was why he couldn't face her. He didn't care what anyone else thought of him, but if she thought he was a 'good for nothing' Bailey he couldn't handle it.

"You have to visit her," Angela insisted.

He hung his head. He knew he was disappointing them. He'd disappointed everyone. "Leave me alone." He turned wishing there was somewhere to hide. Unfortunately, there was nowhere to go to get away, so he went into the stairwell. He collapsed onto one of the steps, covered his face and cried. He loved Ms. Hetty and wished he was in the hospital instead of her. He wished he could take all her pain away, especially since he was the cause. He was a 'no good Bailey' who deserved to die. His mother was right. He was a screw up. He was no different than the rest of the Baileys. Cole quickly wiped his eyes, when he heard footsteps, and turned his face to the wall.

Angela sat beside him and lightly rested a hand on his shoulder. "You have to go see her."

He kept his face turned and shook his head.

"I want you to give her something."

Cole let his shoulders droop then slowly looked at his sister and saw that she held a small stain glass project in her hand.

"It can't be fun being stuck in a hospital, this will brighten it up for her."

Cole sighed, taking the stain glass. It was a picture of a garden. He was so close to making their lives better and he'd failed. There would be no school trip or braces, but he'd at least do this for her.

THE NEXT DAY, he dressed in his best suit. When his mother saw him she laughed. "You're going to a damn hospital not a funeral."

"I want to look my best."

"If you were your father, I'd wonder if you wanted to sweet talk a nurse."

Cole arranged his tie. "No."

"I'm surprised you haven't knocked up a girl yet, but you're still young so there's still time."

"I'm not Dad."

"You better not do that or you're out."

He nodded. He'd heard that since he was five. It wasn't that he wasn't interested in girls, but he had to take care of his family first. And now he had to help Ms. Hetty.

She helped straighten his tie. "Not that it will matter. No matter how fine you look you'll never be one of them."

"I'm not trying to be."

"Then why are you acting as if you're meeting the damn queen or something?"

He knew his mother wouldn't understand, but he wanted to look his best for Ms. Hetty. He wanted to let her know how sorry he was and tell her he would find a way to make things up to her. He took Angela's wrapped gift and left the apartment.

GRANT MET him outside the door to Hetty's hospital room. His gaze swept Cole's worn suit and his mouth quirked in a sneer. "What are you? The undertaker?"

"I came to see Ms. Hetty."

"Sorry. It's family only," he said.

"I just have to give her something."

Grant held out his hand. "I'll give it to her."

"No."

Grant lowered his voice and narrowed his eyes. 'Listen Bailey, I can make your life even more miserable than it is now so you'd better just take my advice and leave."

"I'm not afraid of you."

"That's your mistake. I can--"

"I don't care. I want to see Ms. Hetty."

"Is that Cole?" Hetty called out. "Is that you, my dear?"

"Yes, ma'am," he said boldly meeting Grant's glare. "It's me."

"Are you waiting for an invitation? Come on in."

Cole shoved past Grant.

"There's a hole in your suit," Grant said.

Cole ignored him and walked into the room. Hetty had her own private room. It was filled with flowers. He thought of Angela's gift and knew that it couldn't compete with the grander surrounding him. "I'm so sorry," he said in a rush. "I was sure everything was secure."

"What no hug?" Hetty said lifting her arms out to him.

He gently hugged her. She smelled like lilacs and felt as warm as a summer morning.

"Be careful," Beth snapped, coming into the room. "You've done enough damage. I'm surprised you can show your face."

"I'm sorry, Mrs. Armstrong. I was sure--"

"What have you brought for me?" Hetty said eyeing the package under his arm.

"It's from my sister Angela. She thought you might like it."

"Next time tell her to come." Hetty opened the package then gasped at the item inside. "It's beautiful."

Beth walked over to take a look. "Your sister made this herself?"

Cole nodded with pride. "Yes ma'am."

"We have to put it up." Hetty pointed to the window. "Rest it there so the sunlight can filter through."

Cole did just that and then they all stared at it.

"Hetty," a voice called from the doorway then an elegantly dressed woman walked into the room."You're always causing trouble little sister." The woman stopped and stared at the stain glass. "Oh, where did you get this?"

"It's a gift," Hetty said. She gestured to Cole. "His sister makes them."

"How much?" the woman asked, picking it up to take a closer look.

Hetty gave a reply that left Cole speechless.

"Very well. I'd like to order one. You know that Todd is looking for a student to mentor. Do you think your sister would be interested?" she asked Cole.

"Yes ma'am."

She pulled out her card. "Have her call me."

Cole stared at the card. No one had ever given him their card before. "Yes ma'am."

Grant stood near the door and watched the scene wanting to punch something. This wasn't how it was supposed to be. They were supposed to hate him. "Why are you helping his sister?" he said. "He's the reason you're in here."

"And I forgive him," Hetty said.

"You could have died."

"But I didn't and I think it was meant to be."

Grant widened his eyes incredulous. "Meant to be?"

"Yes, " she said with a bright smile. "All because of the great man above. If I hadn't broken my hip, I wouldn't be here and then Cole's sister wouldn't have given me this picture and my sister wouldn't have seen it and then consider recommending her to Todd. Yes. It's all meant to be. God at work."

"But it wasn't God. I was--" Grant stopped before he implicated himself.

Hetty met his eyes with a keen intelligence that sent a shiver through him. "You were what?"

Grant shook his head, as a trickle of sweat slid down his back. "Nothing. I just think--"

Hetty clapped her hands. "I just had an idea." She turned to Cole. "If my sister has anything to do with it, Angela will be accepted into Todd's program. He's my sister's ex-husband and has an art studio in New York where he mentors aspiring young artists. Angela is very talented and I know he'd enjoy working with her. She would be able to learn and grow her skills while also earning money. " Hetty continued when she saw Cole's hesitation. "I have a house there that I'd love to use again. My husband and I used to go there for vacations. Your sister could live there and she'll need someone to be there with her. I've always wanted to live there but not by myself. I could lookout for her. But we'd need someone to help around the house. Would you like to go too?"

"Oh yes, but..." His words fell away.

"But what?"

"I have another sister."

"There are good schools there. She can come too."

"Mother," Beth said stunned. "What are you saying?"

"'I've got a lot of life left in me and I'm not ready to be put out to pasture. I'm moving."

"I thought you were happy with us. And we can take care of you."

"That's the problem. I don't need you to."

"But these three Bailey kids will--"

"Be the greatest gift to me," she finished.

"Their parents--"

Hetty brushed her concerns aside with a wave of her hand. "I'll make it worth their while."

And she did. Mrs. Bailey was relieved to see her children go so she could have another life. Mr. Bailey wasn't around to argue. Angela was accepted into Todd's exclusive mentorship program, Grace got her braces and enrolled in a private school nearby and Cole felt glad he'd managed to get the life his sisters deserved, leaving the Bailey reputation far behind.

And as they sat in their little house one fall afternoon, Cole thought back to the night he'd imagined spending every holiday with Ms. Hetty and he grinned knowing his Mother's Day wish had come true.

A FORTUNATE MISTAKE

CHAPTER 1

The phone call shattered a beautiful crying fit at
3 a.m. on Christmas Eve. Marina Durosomo
had gone through an entire box of tissues and blown her
nose until it hurt and her red rimmed eyes were dry when
the piercing of the phone invaded her quiet apartment.
She wanted to ignore it, to continue to drown in her
misery and the stinging critique of her now closed bakery
that continued to torment her, but the insistent ringing
wouldn't stop. Who could be calling her now? She didn't
want to hear more bad news. She reluctantly reached for
the phone, slow enough to hope that by the time she
picked up, the person on the other end would hang up.

"Hello?" she said.

"Did I wake you?"

Marina wiped her eyes, recognizing her mother's
voice. She was good at asking questions that didn't need
an answer. If she said 'yes', her mother would apologize
but not really mean it. If she said 'no', her mother would

ask what was wrong and she didn't want to tell her. "I'm fine."

"You sound like you're coming down with a cold."

"I'm fine," she repeated, tossing her empty box of tissues into the recycling bin.

"You don't sound--"

"Mom, what's wrong?"

"I need you to pick up Aunty Helen."

"Aunty who?"

"That's her English name. You won't remember her real one. Besides, you don't know her. She's the mother of a good friend of ours."

Because her mother had about twenty 'good friends' Marina didn't even try to make the connection. It wasn't unusual to have unexpected visitors arrive from Nigeria. They treated their family like a taxi and hotel service, but her mother and father were steeped in the tradition of hospitality and didn't want anything negative said about them back home, even though an ocean separated them. "Okay when will she be here?"

"She's arriving at four-thirty."

"This morning?"

"Yes, why else would I be calling you now? You have an hour and a half to get ready and be over there."

Her mother made it sound so sensible. "Why me?"

"She's coming in at BWI. You're closer to the airport and I have to go to work."

"I work too."

Her mother's responding silence was eloquent. She used to work. She used to have a business she was proud of, but that was all over now. All because of a major recession and a business partner who'd embezzled her funds and disappeared. But no, the truth was her business hadn't failed. She had. There were other bakeries that were flourishing, but the critique had shown a light on all her fears. She just wasn't good enough. Her mother had told her the bakery was a foolish dream, that she should have tried for something more sensible. Her mother would never say 'I told you so', but she didn't have to. Now she would be chauffer to some stranger. This was her punishment. She hated the holidays. Every year they seemed to show her how far she was from the life she wanted. It highlighted another year of grasping for something out of reach.

"What's her flight number?" Marina asked to fill the silence and resigned to her fate.

Her mother told her.

"Can't Wale go?"

"I can't reach him. Hurry, I don't want her waiting there alone. And this will be good for you."

"Good?"

"Yes, to get out of your apartment."

"Mom, I don't need to hear this right now. I just want to sleep."

"You can sleep all you want after you pick her up and settle her in your place."

"My place?"

"Yes, we'll come and get her in the evening."

Marina looked around her messy apartment--the carpet needed a good vacuum, she could spell her name in the dust. After her career imploded she hadn't cared about her surroundings. She didn't want a guest, she didn't want to pretend to celebrate the holidays, she wanted to disappear, but she didn't have a choice.

"What does she look like?" Marina asked opening her closet.

"She's tiny."

Marina waited. When her mother didn't elaborate she rolled her eyes and sighed. "That's all? A tiny black woman?"

"You'll find her," her mother said with impatience. "She'll be looking for you and you will find each other. You're smart." She hung up.

Marina scowled at the phone then disconnected.

At times she hated being a diligent daughter. She wanted to say "Let her wait." Why did this Aunty, what-was-her-name--Helga? Hettie?--have to wait until now to let them know she was arriving? So inconsiderate. She could have called them when she changed flights in Amsterdam. But Marina had learned to keep her thoughts to herself. She had no husband or children to hide behind and now she couldn't even say she had a business to run. She had no life, so she had to do as she was told.

CHAPTER 2

Marina stood in the baggage claim area of Baltimore Washington International feeling like a farmer trying to find a particular blade of grass in a field. Although it wasn't as crowded as a midmorning or late afternoon flight, there were still enough people to get lost in. Marina shoved her hands in her gray wool coat and rocked on her heels. She still couldn't remember the blasted woman's name--Herma? Hilda? Helen? Yes, that was it Helen! But recalling her name was just a small victory. She had no idea how she was supposed to find this woman. Aunty Helen a woman she'd never heard of who was the grandmother of some friend's mother.

Marina was about to give up hope and call her mother when she saw a small woman standing near the wall with a large bag. She wore a brightly colored head-wrap in a pattern she'd never seen before and a well tailored dress that matched. The woman looked composed, as if standing for a portrait--her eighty some years had been kind to her. She had a certain glow that drew Marina to her. She seemed out of place. That had to be her.

Marina made her way over to the woman, confident she'd found the elusive Aunty Helen. Although she wasn't the only one in regional clothes, she was the only one not properly dressed for the cold December weather. At least others sported long coats or gloves, but she only wore her dress, as if she expected to step out into a nice ninety degree sun.

Marina stopped in front of her and smiled."Aunty Helen?"

The woman smiled and her face seemed to glow.

Marina glanced down at her one bag surprised. She'd never picked up someone with so little luggage. "Is that all that you have? Do you need me to help you get the rest?"

She continued to smile.

Marina inwardly groaned. "Please tell me you speak English."

Her smile grew wider.

She softly swore. Why hadn't her mother told her she didn't speak English? That was rare, but the woman looked past eighty so maybe she hadn't had a chance to learn. Unfortunately, her Yoruba wasn't good. She understood it better than speaking it.

In broken Yoruba she attempted to talk to her. "I'm sorry. I'm not good at this. One?" She held up one finger. "Bag?" She pointed to the bag.

The woman blinked and continued to smile.

Marina glanced in the direction of the baggage area and saw that it was empty. "I'm just going to take that as a yes." She turned back to the woman. Things were starting to become a little eerie. She had the bright, trusting nature of a child."Do you have anything warm in there?" She pointed to the bag again.

The woman blinked, but her smile faltered.

Marina pointed outside then hugged herself and shivered. "Cold. You'll be cold. You need something warm." She pointed to the bag again then took the strap. "Can I see?"

The woman released her grip confused.

Marina kneeled and opened the bag. "Please tell me someone had the sense to pack a sweater for you." But she didn't see anything that would be warm enough. Unfortunately, the airport stores were closed. She took off her coat. She had a knit sweater underneath. "You'll have to wear this," she said wrapping it around the woman.

Her bright smile returned and she patted Marina on the cheek. Her hand was remarkably soft and gentle.

The kind gesture made Marina feel like crying all over again. At least someone felt that she was doing something right. Even if it was as simple as keeping them warm. "You're welcome," she said in a brusque tone. She stood. "Come on."

CHAPTER 3

$\mathscr{A}$unty Helen didn't say anything on the drive to Marina's apartment. She stared out at the dark, chilly morning, looking at the bright lights of the highway and the large buildings looming on both sides of the highway. Close to her apartment, Marina stopped at an all-night grocery store and bought another box of tissues and a pair of wool gloves.

When she got back into the car, she rubbed her hands together. "Warm enough?"

Aunty Helen just blinked.

Marina put the gloves in her lap. "You'll need these." She put them on her. "Better?" she said, not expecting a reply and not getting one. Instead Aunty Helen held up her hands, flexed her fingers and smiled.

At home, Marina put Aunty Helen's bag in the hall. She wasn't tired and her guest didn't look so either. Marina mimed holding a bowl and spoon and pretended to eat. "Hungry?" she asked.

Aunty Helen blinked.

She mimed drinking. "Or thirsty?"

The woman blinked again.

Marina sighed. "I'll just give you something okay? And then you can rest on the couch until my mother picks you up and I don't know why I keep talking to you when you don't know what I'm saying."

She put on the kettle for tea then quickly put together a meal of peanut soup she'd recently gotten from her mother.

The woman delve into the meal and again patted her on the cheek, but this time Marina didn't feel like crying. She felt glad she'd been able to make the woman happy. She was clearing up her living room couch to give her a place to nap when her phone rang. She checked the number and sighed when she saw her brother, Wale's, number. "What do you want?"

"To warn you. Mom's upset. You're in big trouble," he said in Yoruba.

"I'm always in trouble," she said in kind.

He laughed then said in English. "Your Yoruba still sucks."

"Shut up, it's not too late for me to give you a lump of coal," she said then hung up the phone, wondering why her brother felt like teasing her. And what could her mother be upset about now? A moment later, her phone rang again. She was about to say something rude when she recognized the number.

"Hi Mom."

"Why didn't you pick up Aunty Helen?" she demanded.

"What do you mean? I did." She looked at the woman

sitting in her kitchen. "She's right here. You could have told me that she didn't speak English."

"What are you going on about? She speaks perfect English. She has a degree from Oxford."

Marina rolled her eyes, not caring where the woman received her degree, though her mother did. She was about to ask why that mattered when her mother continued.

"She just called. Your brother had to go get her."

Marina felt her stomach drop. "That doesn't make any sense. I have Aunty Helen right here. She's eating in my kitchen."

"Oh my god. What have you done?"

Marina's heart started to race and her breathing became shallow. Had she failed again? How could that be? "I did what you told me to. I picked up a woman matching Aunty Helen's vague description. I even asked her her name." Marina paused remembering the incident. She hadn't really asked her name. She'd just said "Aunty Helen?' and the woman smiled and she assumed it was her. "Wait a moment." She ran into the kitchen where the woman was cleaning up her soup with a warm slice of bread. Aunty Helen?"

The woman looked up and smiled.

"You are Aunty Helen?" Marina repeated to make sure.

She continued to smile.

Could she have the same name as the other woman?

"Mom, she seems fine."

"Describe her to me."

"She's small and about eighty something. She didn't

have the proper clothes for the weather and had only one bag."

"Aunty Helen isn't over sixty."

"Why didn't you tell me that before? You said she was the grandmother of one of your friends."

"Not all of my friends are my age. You know that. You should have been more careful. Why are you getting irritated with me? You're the one who picked up the wrong woman. If she were an old woman I would have said Big Mummy not Aunty. Why don't you pay attention to these things? And you should have known I wouldn't send you to pick up someone who doesn't speak English."

Marina rubbed her forehead. Listening to her mother's criticism but only hearing 'you're a failure, you're a failure, you can't do anything right.' "I don't believe this."

"Give her the phone."

Marina held out the phone to her. "Aunty--uh Big Mummy--my mother wants to talk."

The woman nodded and took the phone. She responded with quick fast replies. Her voice was soft and deep, oddly soothing, but Marina couldn't decipher the meaning. The old woman then handed the phone back.

"Why didn't you give her the phone?" her mother demanded when Marina returned to the phone.

Marina squeezed her eyes shut. "What are you talking about? I just did."

"Is she deaf?"

"No. She spoke to you. I heard her. She didn't answer much, but she did speak. I didn't understand her though. It didn't sound like Yoruba. She spoke, but I didn't understand her."

Her mother paused. "You see her? Is she still there?"

"Yes. Where else would she be?"

"Oh no," her mother said in a frightened tone. "I've heard of this but..."

"What?"

"My dear are you sure you're feeling okay? Have you been eating and sleeping properly?"

"Yes, I'm not crazy."

"Lack of sleep can cause hallucinations."

"I'm not hallucinating."

"Or it could be something worse."

"Like what?"

"You picked up a or bloody hell what's the English name for it? I'm not sure they have one exactly. Oh yes...witch."

Don't be daft, she wanted to say, but bit her lip. Her parents believed in both traditional and native religions. "She's not a--I just made a mistake."

"Maybe you should just go back to sleep. If she's still there then get rid of her as fast as you can. Take her to the police and be careful."

CHAPTER 4

Marina took her new arrival to the police station. "I could really use your help," she said to the clerk at the front desk, a woman with finely shaped brows and fading lipstick. "I have an older woman here who's lost. She doesn't seem to speak English and I don't know where to put her."

"Okay. Where is she?"

Marina turned and nodded at the woman, whose feet barely reached the ground. "She's sitting right there."

The clerk looked in the direction Marina gestured to and frowned. "Where?"

"Right there," she pointed, not understanding the other woman's confusion since there was no one else there. "The woman right there."

"What woman?" the clerk said suddenly cautious, licking the rest of her faded lipstick from her mouth.

Marina turned and saw the older woman flash a strange smile. "You don't see her?"

"Do you need somewhere to stay?"

"No, I'm fine."

"Have you been drinking?"

"No."

"Taking anything?"

"I'm perfectly lucid." *At least I think so.* Her mother's suggestion was playing with her thoughts. It couldn't be. How could she have picked up a witch? They didn't exist. Not like this. They weren't invisible. Then why couldn't anyone else see or hear her?

She turned to the woman. "Why are you doing this to me? At least say something."

Her smile remained.

"What have I done wrong to deserve this?"

The clerk cleared her throat. "Why don't you just take a seat? I'll get someone to help you."

Marina spun around and glared at her. "I'm not crazy."

"Of course you're not," the clerk said in an indulgent tone.

Marina was about to take umbrage with her tone when a man came from around the corner. He looked as if he'd had a worse night than she'd had. He hadn't shaved in a while and his tie had the crooked look of a man who just didn't care. If Marina had been in the mood she would have noticed that he was good looking, in a rugged way, but she just didn't care. She wanted to get rid of the old woman and go back to sleep. Or wake up from this nightmare, whichever was faster.

"Idris what's the name of the local shelter?" the clerk asked.

"It's going to be pretty full," he said. "What's that other lady here for?"

The clerk stared at him stunned.

Marina jumped with joy, wanting to grab his sleeve but refraining. She wasn't imagining things. "You see her too?"

He sent her an odd look. "Of course I see her. She's sitting right there. How could I miss her?"

The clerk shook her head. "Idris you've had a long night."

"I know."

"There's no one there."

"Maybe you need a rest. It's two to one."

"There's one way to decide this." The clerk took out her phone and took a picture. Then she grinned with triumph. "I'm right." She turned the image to them. They saw the wall and an empty chair.

Marina turned to the woman then the image on the tiny screen. "I don't believe this."

"There's something wrong with your camera," Idris said.

The clerk took the phone and tucked it away. "It's Christmas Eve and it's a crazy night, weird things happen. I think you two should just go home. "

The older woman leaped to her feet. "Yes, it's time," she said in perfect English. Then she grabbed Marina's hand and Idris's.

"What are you doing?" Idris said.

"You speak English?" Marina said at the same time.

They both looked at the woman then each other with a mixture of fear and awe then their world went black.

CHAPTER 5

When Idris Helmond came to, he didn't know how to feel. One moment he was thinking about closing a case on the brutal beating of a gas station attendant and finding the right gift to make his girlfriend, Deena, happy. She was pissed about something, but that wasn't new. She was always pissed about something and she wouldn't tell him why, she'd only let him know he was the cause. Then he'd seen the pretty young woman trying to find shelter for an older woman who looked strangely cunning.

He didn't know where he was or what to think. He looked around him and saw the neat road and manicured lawns of a neighborhood. The place felt familiar. He looked around and spotted a house--It was his sister's house. Beautifully decorated for the holidays. But he knew it wasn't like that now. That house was no longer hers. The scene was from three years ago. He shook his head in rising dread and took a hasty step back. "No, no. What are we doing here?"

"You have to be here," the older woman said.

"No, I don't. I know what happens. I don't need to be here. Let's go."

"Idris."

He threw up his hand, his voice in a near panic. "I said I don't want to be here."

"What is this place?" Marina asked.

"It doesn't matter, let's go." But the woman wouldn't release her hold and she had the strength to keep him there. "Get us out of here whoever--or whatever you are," he said in his best 'or you'll regret this' tone.

But the older woman didn't release him.

He turned and saw a woman march up to the front door as if on a mission. She flipped through the many keys on her keychain before she got the right one. She placed the key in the lock then turned the handle with an angry twist. "No. Don't go in there. Please." He turned to the older woman, feeling as if he could no longer breathe. "Make her stop."

"I can't."

"Then why did you bring me here?"

"Haven't you been playing this scene over in your mind for three years? Haven't you already remembered and replayed every detail? Isn't this the reason you won't see your nephews? Why you make excuses not to visit your parents every holiday season? You're here because this is where you're stuck. This is where you stopped your life too. Your sister got twenty-five to life, but you're living a life sentence by staying in a job you hate because it makes your parents proud. Staying in a relationship that is soulless. You chose this. When are you going to get past this moment? A moment that will never change?"

"She shouldn't have had keys to his place. Why did it have to happen? She was my baby sister and I couldn't stop her. "

"No. She was a woman who'd made a choice."

"I gave her the gun to protect herself."

"She used it for something else. Your sister couldn't except that her ex had remarried, that he'd created a new life for himself. Just like you, she couldn't move on. She was convicted because she hadn't snapped. She decided to pick up the kids early. She decided to catch her ex with his new love and she decided to shoot them both dead."

They heard a scream and then three pops.

"You couldn't have stopped it," the older woman said.

Idris fell to his knees, losing all strength, as if he'd been shot too. The awful part was the guilt. Her husband had been his best friend. He'd felt the loss from the divorce too. His sister had been married to Nathanial for ten years and he'd been a good father to their two sons. He'd been someone Idris had admired. He'd expected Nathanial to be his best man one day. He'd seen them as the perfect couple until the cracks began to show.

He remembered his brother-in-law complaining about his sister's drinking and shopping sprees. He remembered Nathanial getting full custody of the children. Idris understood the judge's ruling, his sister had become unstable, but he still had divided loyalties, even though it was best for the boys. His parents had remained blind wanting to see their precious little girl as the victim and Nathanial as the villain. But he knew it wasn't as black and white as that. Just like his nephews, his world had been shattered that day. He'd buried someone who'd been like a brother and lost his sister too. She was still bitter, even in prison. She still blamed the system for not understanding her rage. His parents blamed him for not seeing the signs sooner. For somehow not stopping it.

"The season had nothing to do with her choice," the older woman said.

"Really?" he said with a sneer. "You know the rates of murders go up around the holidays?"

"Was it the holidays that put the liquor down her throat or the gun in her hand?"

"She snapped because she felt so alone," Idris said trying to rationalize something he knew he couldn't. "She felt disconnected. It's a season that feeds discontentment. Domestic violence cases practically sky rocket. A time of good cheer my ass. People find even more reasons to hate each other."

"Remember when you and Nathanial took your nephews sledding? Remember the time when you both laughed at the instructions for putting together a racecar track? You had joy. That joy was real. It's okay to love your sister and hate what she did. Your friend wouldn't want you to throw away all the good times just for this moment. You have to get past this."

"I don't know how," he said his voice raw. He glanced at the younger woman, who stood motionless beside the other woman, wondering why he'd chosen to share this nightmare with her.

"You can do it by looking at this place one last time. And saying goodbye."

"My parents blame me and his parents won't talk to me."

"You shut Nathanial's parents out of your life as much as you have your nephews. And they miss you. Don't let the memory of their father die. You don't have to replace him. But make his life mean more than his death. Don't let your sister's bitterness rob you too."

A purple fog quickly swept over the scene and soon they stood in front of Nathanial's grave. A light dusting of snow fell from the blanket of white clouds, but Idris didn't feel cold. He didn't feel anything. He brushed the snow from the headstone then gathered some and let it melt between his fingers. He remembered introducing Nathanial to his sister and the instant attraction between them. He remembered his sister telling him about their first date. He remembered their wedding day and visiting the hospital when Nathanial held their first son and the pride and joy on his face.

Tears filled and stung his eyes as he recalled the fights, the tense phone calls, the divorce proceeding and then his sister's conviction. Both he and Nathanial had been detectives, determined to help and serve others, but hadn't been able to fix their own lives. Idris tasted the tears though he didn't feel them streaming down his face. 'I'm so sorry," he said, then he felt the cold against his skin, the wetness on his cheeks. He felt his loss, his rage and his despair.

"He's forgiven you," the old woman said. "He wants you to know that. Now you have to forgive yourself."

Idris wiped his tears then fell to his knees feeling like a broken man. "I can't."

"Because you're afraid. You're afraid that if it couldn't go right for him, it won't for you. So you won't even try. But you're wrong. You can have the life you want. You know Nathanial knew there were signs early on that the relationship wouldn't work. He told you some of them but he chose to ignore them. I'm not saying he's responsible, but there are gray areas that none of you could see. Some you didn't want to see."

Idris nodded. "I know."

"Now say the name of his favorite holiday song."

"No."

"Say it, then say goodbye."

He shook his head. "It's stupid."

"Say it anyway."

He sighed. "I Want a Hippopotamus for Christmas."

Marina giggled then covered her mouth embarrassed, but Idris heard it anyway and couldn't help a smile. He'd forgotten she was there and he felt awkward that she'd seen him at such a fragile time. He was used to keeping his emotions bottled up, but when he looked at her, he didn't feel that she was judging him and that made his awkwardness disappear. Made him glad he wasn't alone. "The idiot," he said with fondness. "He loved that song and knew all the words. He'd hum it just to annoy me."

"Sounds like a fun guy."

"He was. He loved the holidays. Everything about it."

Marina kneeled beside him and tentatively took his hand, half expecting him to pull away. "I'm sorry."

He squeezed her hand and released a deep shuddering breathe, as if he'd been holding it a long time. "Thanks."

"Do you really hate your job?" she asked.

"Yes, every single day I feel like I'm dying."

"Then why don't you change it?"

He sent her a look of surprise. "You think it's that easy?"

"No, but it's better than feeling like this."

"Tell her what you want," the old woman said.

He stood and dusted snow from his trousers although he didn't need to. Although the ground was powered with snow, his trousers remained dry. "No."

"Are you afraid to?"

"Yes."

"Tell her later then." The old woman turned to Marina. "Now it's your turn."

"I guess I don't have a choice," she said with a grimace before their world went black.

CHAPTER 6

After seeing Idris's past, Marina prepared herself for a painful holiday memory. So when she saw the sight of her old bakery kitchen she couldn't help her surprise. She stared at the sight of the woman she'd been four years ago. The kitchen was small, all her new equipment that Eli would encourage her to purchase hadn't filled the room yet. She saw herself stirring something in a bowl and humming. She then scooped the contents into a tube and decorated cookies with a flair of fun. Her efforts weren't perfect, but she didn't seem to mind. Marina gaped at her younger self with wonder. She didn't remember even being that happy.

"What are we doing here?" Marina asked. "I already know I'm going to fail. I already know this isn't what I'm meant to do."

The old woman held up one finger. "Just wait."

Marina folded her arms, feeling impatient. She didn't want to wait. She wanted to leave. She wanted to go back to sleep and forget this day ever happened. She was about to comment to the fact when Eli walked into the room. Eli the man she'd thought she'd loved and who she'd thought loved her and her dreams. The man who'd told her he'd support her through thick and thin. The one who'd later embezzle her funds and leave her heart broken.

"What are you doing?"

"Working on a new icing."

He frowned "You're still trying that?"

"I want to make it work."

"You're wasting your time. Why don't you just focus on what will make money?"

For the first time Marina noticed how he hadn't greeted her and how much he didn't look pleased. Why hadn't she seen that before? He was only about making money. He didn't care what she did. He didn't care about her passion. She loved baking, she'd forgotten about that. She'd let him douse her hopes and leave an empty shell.

But the younger version of herself didn't know this. She gave him a taste of the icing.

He made a face and shook his head. "It's still not up to standard. You know you're no good at this. I told you to stick with simple things. Why won't you listen?"

"I wanted to give customers a new experience."

"This isn't a culinary institute. You're not making art. Just bake cookies and cakes and you'll be in the black instead of the red. Now let's go."

Marina saw the light in her eyes dim.

"Who is this jerk?" Idris said.

"The man I thought I'd marry," Marina said.

"Oh, sorry."

"Me too."

She saw her younger self watch Eli leave the kitchen and then she took all her experiments and dumped them into the trash.

"That was the moment you let him steal your dream," the old woman said.

Marina let her hands fall to her sides. "My dream failed. I failed. The business flopped. Even if he hadn't taken the money he was right, I was no good."

"But you were getting better. You stopped trying. You listened to him when you should have ignored him. He didn't support you. He lied to you and you believed his lies. What if you'd kept experimenting and one of them worked? You started to make your business just about money and not about joy. That was when you gave up on your dream. Your dream never gave up on you." The old woman pointed to the trash bin. "This is the moment you failed."

Marina twisted her lips and shrugged. "It's too late now."

The old woman took Marina's hand and patted it. "You're too young to start speaking like an old woman. Even if you were my age it wouldn't be too late to live with joy. To try. To dream." The old woman looked at Idris. "Are you ready to tell her what you've always wanted to do?"

"No."

She sighed.

"Why won't you tell me?" Marina asked. "We'll never see each other again. Are you afraid because you'll fail like I did?"

He shoved his hands in his pockets and looked away.

Marina looked at the old woman. "I don't understand any of this." She glanced around the kitchen that was no longer hers. A past that still caused her pain. "Why are you showing us things we can't change?"

"Because that's the point. You can't change the past, but the future is yours. You don't have to be stuck here. The holidays are full of presents. Not just the gifts given to each other, but the moments you inhabit every day. They matter. The choices you make matter. Make your presents matter, then the future will belong to you. You just have to believe it."

Marina bit her lip then squinted at her. "What are you?"

"Does it matter?"

"Why couldn't I understand you before?"

"Because you weren't ready to."

"Why us?"

The old woman kissed her teeth with annoyance. "You ask such silly questions. Why not you? If I am a spirit or a ghost or your imagination does it matter? Those questions aren't important. The important question is: What will you do next?"

"Will we remember any of this?"

She just smiled.

Idris rested his hands on his hips. "What should we do next?"

Her smile just widened.

"I think that's all she'll tell us," Marina said. "This is what she did to me when we first met."

"I guess it's a sign that our journey is coming to an end."

"Yes." Marina glanced at his tie and had a strange urge to straighten it, but resisted. She lifted her gaze to his face. He had a nice face and she wished she could know him better. After Eli's betrayal, she hadn't wanted to know another man. "Whatever happens, good luck to you. I hope that you'll see your nephews this year."

"And you should keep baking, if it makes you happy."

"It does." She tilted her head to the side. "And what did you always want to do?"

This time he only smiled but for the first time she saw a twinkle in his eye.

"Fine, don't tell me. Good luck with that too."

"Thanks."

The old woman took both their hands and they shared a look--this time with hope and anticipation--then the world went black.

CHAPTER 7

The phone call shattered a beautiful dream at 3a.m. on Christmas Eve. Marina groggily reached for the phone hoping that it would stop ringing by the time she picked up. It didn't.

"Hello?"

"I'm sorry to wake you," her mother said. "But I need you to pick up Uncle Sola."

"Who?"

"Uncle Sola. He'll be arriving at BWI and--"

"Mom I can't keep doing this."

"I know and I feel bad but I know you're off all week."

"Off?" Was she trying to be funny? She wasn't off. She didn't have a job.

"Yes, you and the boys are going to Delaware. Just this quick favor and I won't do it again." She gave the flight number and description then hung up.

Delaware? Boys? Her words vaguely made sense but then they didn't make sense at all. Her mind felt as though it was between a dream and a wake state.

"What was that about?" a deep voice said beside her.

Marina froze. She knew that voice, but yet she didn't know it. And what was he doing in her bed? She slowly turned to him. Idris. Not the sad, tired Idris from the police station. He looked sleepy, but happy.

She pushed her sheets away. "I have to go pick someone up from the airport."

He frowned and put the sheets back. "No, you're not."

"My mother."

"Give me the phone."

"But--"

He reached across her, grabbed the phone and dialed. "Hi Mom. Sorry she can't make it. Tell him to take a taxi and I'll pay for the tab. Yes, I know. I don't care. Then get Wale to do it. Yes. Okay, bye." He disconnected and handed her the phone.

Marina gripped the phone in two hands. "What did she say?"

"Relax. You don't have to go."

He'd called her mother 'Mom'. Yes, because he was her husband. That felt right. Yes, they were married. Why had she ever imagined him sad? And she'd never been in a police station. Where had that thought come from? The dream state faded and everything became clear. They'd been married a year. He used to be a detective and now he was a real estate developer, raising his two nephews. She did catering: Sweet desserts. She wasn't making lots of money but she was happy and he always let her practice her experiments on him and the boys loved to be in the kitchen with her. She suddenly remembered snow ball fights and searching for a tree. But most of all she remembered meeting him one Christmas day.

He'd taken his nephews to a birthday party a friend had invited her to cater and their eyes met over a row of cupcakes and for her it felt like she'd known him from somewhere. Like they'd known each other forever. She still felt that way.

Marina settled back under the warm sheets. There was a question that niggled her mind. She didn't know why, but for some reason she wanted to know the answer. She had to. "What have you always wanted to do?"

Idris was slow to answer and at first she thought he may have fallen back asleep.

He hadn't. He felt as if someone had asked him that question before and he'd had a hard time answering. But now he wanted to. He looked around the cozy bedroom knowing his nephews were safe and asleep in their beds, the presents were under the tree ready to be opened. He could already taste the maple syrup covered waffles Marina would make for breakfast. He looked at his wife, his friend, unsure he could put into words all they'd asked for. He'd wanted to follow his heart and take care of his nephews, build a business that would support his family and find a woman he wasn't afraid to love. One he could trust. A woman who'd love him just as he was.

Idris drew her close, amazed that he'd gotten all that he'd ever dreamed. "This," he said then tenderly placed his lips against hers.

And the next morning on top of the Christmas tree,

Marina saw an angel that wasn't the same one she'd put there several weeks ago. It didn't have wings, instead it wore a brightly colored headwrap, matching dress and a big smile.

ABOUT THE AUTHOR

Dara Girard, an award-winning, national bestselling author of more than fifty novels and many short stories, from romance to suspense, loves telling stories.

Born in the US to immigrant parents, Dara enjoys pulling from her Jamaican, British, Nigerian heritage and exposure to various cultures to bring what reviewers and fans call "vivid emotional stories" to life. She is best known for her popular Henson Series, the mysterious Clifton Sisters, and the fun Black Stockings Society.

Visit her website to sign up for her newsletter and get sneak peeks, monthly updates on new releases, and special offers.

For more information visit
www.daragirard.com

www.ingramcontent.com/pod-product-compliance
Lightning Source LLC
Chambersburg PA
CBHW030351200726
48286CB00013B/1081